FRONT PAGE
Love

MONTANA SKIES

Book 2

FRONT PAGE
Love

PAIGE LEE
ELLISTON

Revell

Grand Rapids, Michigan

© 2006 by Paige Lee Elliston

Published by Fleming H. Revell
a division of Baker Publishing Group
P.O. Box 6287, Grand Rapids, MI 49516-6287

Printed in the United States of America

Library of Congress Cataloging-in-Publication Data
Elliston, Paige Lee, 1943–
    Front page love / Paige Lee Elliston.
        p.   cm.—(Montana skies ; bk. 2)
    ISBN 0-8007-5940-0 (pbk.)
    1. Women journalists—Fiction. 2. Montana—Fiction. I. Title.
PS3605.L4755F76 2006
813'.6—dc22   2005027035

1

Julie Downs stood sweating and acutely uncomfortable in front of the Coldwater, Montana, *News-Express* building. The time-temperature sign on the bank down the street read 104 degrees. The building offered no shade, and the sun hung low in the sky, flexing its midday muscles.

Julie felt her blouse begin to stick to her back as she stood on the sidewalk. Her long hair, a sun-kissed hue of blond, had always been a source of secret pride to her. But now she felt as if a slightly damp mop had sprouted on her head. She tapped a western boot impatiently—which reminded her how hot her feet were. The sidewalk was radiating heat like a short-order grill. A headline ran through her mind:

Reporter Bursts into Flames Awaiting Ride in Cop Car

Julie wasn't good at waiting—particularly waiting for meatball interviews on topics that were of little interest to her and, she suspected, her readers.

She glanced at her watch, then looked down Main Street. A half block away, a realtor was placing his sign on the boarded-up front window of what had been a cute little candy and ice cream store. Farther down the street, beyond where Julie could see, were other closed shops and small businesses, operations that depended on the discretionary income of the residents of Coldwater.

Julie sighed. Many of those residents were farmers and ranchers, and the previous summer—the first of the year-and-a-half-long drought—had been a disaster. The merciless sun had turned rich, lush pasture to arid expanses of dirt and burned grass, and melted weight from the cattle that depended on those pastures. And the horse industry, large and robust in Montana for many years, now found sales low and feed prices high.

Julie checked her watch again: 12:09.

New Cop Unable to Tell Time—
Ace Reporter Melts on Sidewalk

Like this guy has something more important to do, she thought. *Coldwater's a real hotbed of crime. Just last week, the president of the reading circle was found to have a two-day fine against her at the public library. And the week before, Howie Warden's Labrador retriever ate a darning egg belonging to a neighbor . . .*

She stepped back to the doors, the tall, dark glass panels of which made a good substitute for a mirror, and inspected her image critically. Definitely a bad hair day—there was no doubt about that. She was tall—five foot nine—and in her own mind scrawny, or at least lanky. Her figure was more girlish than womanly. She leaned closer, looking at her

6

features. Her face was pleasant enough to look at, and her teeth were white and even in a full, but not quite sensuous, mouth. *Not too bad for a thirty-six-year-old,* she thought.

The squeal of tires and the throaty, powerful roar of a large engine brought Julie back to the curb. A glinting new Ford, purchased for and donated to the department by the grateful rancher parents of a toddler who wandered off and was brought home quickly and safely by the police, slid around the corner in a four-wheel drift, straightened, and rocketed in Julie's direction, its massive power plant howling. The vehicle was polished so highly that the reflecting sunlight made it hard to look at.

The Ford skidded to a stop in front of Julie. The driver's door swung open, and Patrol Officer Kenneth Townsend climbed out of the cruiser and stepped to its front.

Julie appraised him quickly, from his poster-boy smile to his obviously tailor-made uniform and black boots that were at least as well shined as his cruiser. He was darkly tanned, tall and lean, and bore himself with an almost military posture. Good looking, she decided, and well aware of that fact.

"Ken Townsend," he said, sounding like Sean Connery saying, "Bond—James Bond." Julie wanted to giggle. She'd heard the new officer was a Hollywood version of a cop. "Sorry I'm a minute late, Ms. Downs. I had some business to take care of."

Julie didn't say anything.

"Uhhh . . ." Officer Townsend said, his face turning red, "you are Julie Downs, aren't you?"

She wanted very badly to say no.

"Yes, I am." She shifted her eyes to the cruiser. "This is the super car, right?"

The officer smiled broadly, proudly. "You betcha. Ford Interceptor. She'll run top end over 140. Five-speed gearbox, 456 cubic inches, handling package, high capacity disk brakes—"

Julie stopped the spiel with a wave of her hand. "I got a brochure from your captain. Let's go for a ride and talk a bit."

"Sure, let's do that." The officer motioned with his hand to the passenger side, took the few steps to his own door, and dropped himself back into the car behind the wheel. Julie stood still. Townsend's face reddened again, and he got out of his cruiser and walked around to the passenger door, opening it for her.

Why did I do that? she chided herself. *After all, it's the new millennium. I'm capable of opening a door.*

Julie hooked her shoulder harness as the cop walked back around the car and got inside once again. He seemed completely at home in the driver's seat, and his hands fell naturally to the steering wheel. The image of a jet fighter pilot flashed in Julie's mind. *Not a bad impression,* she thought. A cluster of chrome switches and a scanner/radio rested on the dark dashboard. The upright shotgun resting on its stock in a clamp set slightly to the left of the instrument pod, within easy reach, set off the functionality of the vehicle.

Officer Townsend started the engine, snicked the shift lever into first gear, and left the curb with tires smoking and motor screaming like a wild beast. He slam-shifted into second, burning the tires once again.

"Enough," Julie said over the roar.

"Ma'am?"

"Enough! I know it's fast. Let's just ride for a few minutes like normal human beings, and then you can drop me off. OK?"

The officer looked confused for a moment—and a little disappointed. "Sure. Thing is, I never know when I'll have to call on the powers of that awesome engine to—"

"I understand," Julie interrupted. "But let's talk about you. I'd like my readers to get to know you." She'd taken a pad and pen from her purse and wrote her first line on a fresh page: "Hollywood—awesome engine—could be good cop when he calms down (??)." She looked at the page again.

Nuts. It's not this guy's fault that I'm hot, sweaty, and irritable, and that my hair looks like an oiled haystack. I gotta cut him some slack.

"Tell me, Officer," she said, smiling somewhat larger than she was feeling, "how did you get into law enforcement?"

The officer responded to both the smile and the question as he drove beyond the end of Main Street and out into the open land, edging the cruiser up to a relatively moderate sixty-five miles per hour. Julie took an occasional note, fully realizing that the computer background sweep of Ken she'd done earlier gave her all the data she needed for her article.

Officer Townsend told her about his early desire to be a cop, his failure to be accepted by the FBI, his dozen years

9

as a private investigator, and his training at the Montana State Police Academy. His spiel sounded rehearsed to Julie's practiced ears, almost devoid of contractions, employing terms such as "did not" and "would have" rather than the far more common "didn't" and "would've."

The poor guy memorized this speech.

"Married?" she asked idly. The computer data showed he was thirty-five years old and single.

"No," he said. "I guess I never really found the time. PI work takes lots of hours, mostly at night, when normal people are dating." After a moment he asked, "How about you?"

"Nope," Julie answered. "Never been. It's a cliché, I guess, but in a sense I'm married to my work. I love what I do, and I love my life outside my job. I have a good—a great—horse, and I'm a barrel racer."

"I've seen barrel racing on TV but never live," Officer Townsend said. "It looks like lots of fun."

"You'll have to come to the Montana finals at the end of the summer. You'll see good riding and top horses."

"I'll do that," he said, and his tone of voice clearly indicated that he would.

Julie shifted in her seat and moved her boots to a more comfortable position. As she did so, she glanced downward and noticed the edge of a cellophane bag shoved behind the police monitor. Before even thinking of restraining herself, she leaned forward and tugged the bag free of its hiding place. The bag contained Tootsie Roll Pops, and about half of them were gone.

"Aha!" she said, shaking the bag. "And don't tell me you carry these for kids, Officer."

His face flushed pink. He slowed, downshifted, and pulled to the shoulder of the road, still rolling as he swung into a U-turn and headed back to Coldwater, accelerating easily to sixty-five miles per hour.

"OK," he began. "You found the evidence. I guess I have to tell you the rest." He paused for a moment, and then his voice dripped with artificial emotion. "I . . . I've been addicted to Tootsie Pops since I was about ten years old. Until now, no one knew about it . . . except my dentist."

Julie laughed. "Your secret is safe with me, Ken," she said. "In fact, I'll let you in on an even darker secret. With me, it's Snickers bars—and I mean the full-size jobs, not the tiny ones sold around Halloween. I'm powerless over them."

"Wow," Ken breathed. "Snickers are hard core, Julie." He seemed to ponder for a long moment. "At times—and I'm not proud of this—I've scarfed down a Three Musketeers or even a few Atomic Fireballs. Once, when I was younger, a pair of PayDays. But Snickers bars . . ." His voice trailed off to silence.

Julie laughed again, and then they were laughing together, like grade school kids at recess. Julie noticed that they'd slipped past the "Ms. Downs" and "Officer Townsend" phase to a natural comfort with each other's first names.

Julie watched the parched fields and dusty pastures pass by her window. The ride back to the *News-Express* building seemed to pass too quickly. Ken pulled to the curb, and Julie unsnapped her shoulder belt.

11

"Thanks for the ride and your time, Ken. You'll like my article."

"I'm sure I will. Hey, would you like to grab a cup of coffee or something in a few days?" His smile was dazzling, and his eyes warm and friendly. Julie was no stranger to being hit on by guys, but this felt different. *If you can't trust a cop, who can you trust?*

She returned his smile. "I'd like that. Give me a call here"—she nodded at the *News-Express* building—"or at home. My number is listed."

Julie eased out of the cruiser and closed the door with a solid, new-car *thunk*. She walked to the big doors of the front entrance to the newspaper office. Behind her she heard Ken drive off—quietly, with no screeching of tires.

Well, well, well . . . She grinned to herself like a cat in sunshine.

The blast of almost frigid air inside the building was heavenly, and Julie stood just inside the door, reveling in it. Even the dozen or so steps from the cruiser to the office had exposed her to the sun and caused sweat to break on her forehead and arms. She sighed.

"You OK, Jules?" a voice asked. "You're lookin' lost in space."

Julie smiled at co-reporter Mandy Fairwell. "Out on an interview," she said. "It's so hot the rattlesnakes are wearing sun bonnets."

"You got that new cop piece, right? The cute guy?"

"That's where I was just now."

Mandy took a step closer. "How'd it go?"

"OK," Julie said. "He talked a lot about his car that'll go a bazillion miles an hour. Seems like a nice guy, though."

"Mmm. Married?"

Julie's smile answered her friend's question.

"Ohh—Nancy is looking for you," Mandy remembered.

"What's up?"

"I don't know. She seems like she's all wound up about something." Mandy looked at her watch. "I gotta get out on the town council meeting. Catch you later, OK?"

Julie began to answer but then realized she would only be talking to her friend's back. After a moment, she headed to the newsroom, wondering what Nancy Lewis, her managing editor, needed from her.

Nancy was new to the paper; she'd come to Coldwater shortly before the drought began. The absentee owners, a communications conglomerate, had a pair of options at that time: either cut their losses and dump the paper or get someone into the front office who could bring the paper back to profitability. Nancy Lewis had the credentials, the experience, and the talent the owners wanted. At only forty-five years of age she'd yanked one small-town paper from the edge of bankruptcy and had guided two others from throwaways to well-read and respected publications.

Julie ducked into the ladies room and stood in front of the mirror. She sighed, rearranged some wandering lengths of hair, and left, thankful that she didn't use makeup beyond a bit of lipstick. Mascara and foundation would have long since melted.

Nancy's door was open, and she was sitting behind her

13

desk. As ever, the surface of the desk was pristine and un-cluttered, an uncapped Mt. Blanc fountain pen centered on a fresh legal pad. Both the in and out baskets were empty. She waved Julie in and motioned her to sit.

Julie chose the armed chair centered in front of the desk rather than the small couch to the side. She noticed Nancy's perfume as she sat and set her shoulder bag on the floor. The scent was light but exotic—reminding Julie of spice and, for some reason, wildflowers.

Nancy smiled. No one would refer to her as beautiful, although her features were even and her eyes lively and open. The word that sprang to Julie's mind was *patrician*—Nancy projected a presence that quietly demanded attention no matter where she was or what she was doing.

"How are things, Julie?" she asked. Her voice was smooth and well modulated, with the slightest touch of the South that tempered the hardness of her *r*'s.

"Fine. No complaints."

Nancy's smile broadened. "None?"

"Well, you know how it is," Julie admitted. "Not much going on around here—except the drought."

"I'm not completely sure about that," Nancy said. "Do you know specifically why the police department hired the new man?"

"The way I heard it," Julie said, "is that the chief was dead set against it, said he didn't need a new officer and that the force was fully staffed. It was the town council that demanded the PD bring on the new guy—said they'd find the money to pay and equip him. The donated cruiser certainly helped."

"As it turned out, the council was right. Violent crime—fights, threats, theft, even some cattle rustling—has gone way up in the last six to eight months. That bar out at the end of Main Street—the Bulldogger—is opening at 8:00 in the morning now, and doing lots of business. Farmers, cowhands, farm help, other guys out of work have been spending too much time there, getting liquored up and arguing. There was a bad fight a couple of nights ago—and a stabbing."

Julie nodded her head. "I've heard lots of rumors. Of course, that place has always been a dump. The town has even tried to close it down a few times."

Nancy nodded. "Yeah, but it's worse now. And it's not only the bar. There are too many people with nothing to do, too many people worrying about losing their farm equipment, their cars, their land, and even their homes, to the banks."

"It's the drought—"

"Exactly," Nancy interrupted. "It's the drought. Records show this one is the worst since the Great Depression. That's scary, no?"

Julie nodded. "I talked with Cyrus Huller in the café last week. You know him, right? Anyway, he remembers the Depression. He told me how his family barely survived it—how he got smacked if he came back without a possum or squirrel or woodchuck for each bullet his dad gave him to hunt with. Cyrus said they ate anything—including snake."

"I know Cyrus. He's a wonderful source of history. I'm

15

really pleased that you spoke with him—and I think you'll be sitting down with him again quite soon."

"Yeah? Why's that?"

Nancy leaned slightly forward in her chair, her hands folded on her desk. "This drought is like a living thing. It's attacking the people here, and it's draining the blood from them. It's scaring them."

Julie didn't quite know how to respond, so she sat quietly, her eyes locked with those of her managing editor.

"You've done great work here, Julie. Your column has been working well. Your features and bit stories get read and talked about. The horse people, the cattlemen, the farmers, the businesspeople all trust you."

Julie could feel heat in her face. "That's kind of you to say, Nancy. I love the people and I love Coldwater, and I guess maybe that shows in my writing."

Nancy leaned back a bit. "OK. You're wondering now why the big 'attagirl,' right? Why'd Lewis drag me in here to tell me that I walk on water?"

"Well . . . it's great to hear, but . . ."

"Here's the deal," Nancy said. "I'm assigning you to an open-ended series on the drought in Montana and the effect it's having on the people in the Coldwater part of the state. I don't want fluff or sugarcoating. I want—I demand—in-depth interviews and from-the-heart writing. I want the perspectives and attitudes of the people you talk to, but I want yours too. I want to hear them talk to me through your words." She paused for a moment. "What do you think so far?"

"I . . . I uhh . . ." Julie stuttered.

"I hope I can anticipate more articulate phrasing in the articles, Ms. Downs," Nancy said sternly. Then she laughed. "You'll report only to me on the series. I'm taking you off everything else, and I've already written an editorial telling readers why your column will be discontinued while you're on this assignment."

"I'm really stunned—and grateful, Nancy. I'll give you my best work. I can promise you that."

"I know you will. I'm afraid there'll be a couple of noses out of joint when I announce the assignment, but this series is something I believe in. I had to give it to my top performer." She leaned back in her chair. Julie waited for her to go on.

"I've never changed my basic policy of what a newspaper should do or be. I've studied what happens at small presses during times of peril. I've read thousands of dailies and weeklies from the States and from Great Britain. The press in London was magnificent during the bombings, and so was the press here during the Depression." She waved her hand as if whisking away smoke. "My point is that our readers depend on us. It's our job—our obligation—to tell them what's going on, whether good or bad. The truth may frighten them, but it won't cause a panic, as irresponsible publishing can do. I want you to pick this drought apart, Julie. Talk to anyone you care to or need to, go wherever you want, see what you feel the need to see." Nancy waited a moment and then added, "Give us some hope, if you can. But tell us the truth."

"There's always hope," Julie said, almost without being aware she'd spoken.

"Maybe so," Nancy mused. She paused a moment, then said, "There's one other thing, and this is off the record. What do you know about our chief of police?"

"Well, Ross Craig's a fixture in Coldwater—he's been in office forever. He doesn't have many friends on the city council, but the people seem to accept him." She hesitated for a moment and then went on. "I recall there were allegations of election problems last time he was elected, but nothing ever came of it."

Nancy nodded. "Anything you hear about Chief Craig, bring to me, OK?"

"Sure. But may I ask why? What's going on?"

"Nothing, maybe—at least right now. Remember, I'm still the new kid on the block. I need all the information I can get on the old-timers."

Nancy ended the meeting with another smile. "OK. I want two thousand or more words per week, beginning ten days from today. Check in with me every couple of days or so. Any questions?"

Julie stood, her legs a tad shaky, and reached across the desk. Nancy stood too and took Julie's hand as if they were captains of industry sealing a multibillion-dollar deal.

"Go," Nancy said. "I've got work to do."

"Wow," Julie mouthed silently to herself as she walked dazedly to her cubicle. She dropped into her chair, clicked on her computer more from habit than intent, and stared at the icons that appeared on her screen but didn't really see them.

This is what I trained for—an important story, a series that will have a real impact on the lives of my readers. The drought is on everyone's mind. Nancy's right. People—all of us—are nervous. Maybe through my words and pictures I can lessen that fear a bit, or offer a little hope, or . . .

The tiny, tinny notes of a Bach concerto coming from her cell phone buried somewhere in her large leather purse brought Julie back to the *Express* newsroom. She had to clear her throat twice before speaking.

"Julie Downs."

"Julie—Danny Pulver."

"Oh, hi, Danny. What's up?"

"I'm at your place with Drifter. I've examined him, and I don't see any shoeing or gait problem. Those marks you're seeing above his shoes . . ."

Julie mentally shifted gears. She'd called Danny Pulver, the local vet, to look at some abrasions at the front heels of her Quarter Horse gelding, Drifter. "I thought he might be striking himself with the toes of his rear shoes."

"No, it's not a gait interference thing. Actually, it's a fairly common problem in very dry parts of the country. There's a long, technical name for it, but the cowboys call it 'scratches.' Drifter doesn't have it too bad, but you're going to have to apply a salve twice a day, morning and night, until it goes away."

Julie released a deep breath of relief. "Sure. No problem. Should I wrap his legs or anything else?"

"No. We want the air to get to the scratches. Don't worry about this, though. He's fine. The salve will take care of it."

"Thanks, Danny. Can you leave some salve or can I get it at the pharmacy?"

"Well, no. The thing is, I have to mix some up for you at my clinic. No one I know of makes the stuff commercially." He laughed. "Actually, it's a formula an old rodeo hand I knew in veterinary school gave me. I need an eye of newt, some wolfbane . . ."

Julie laughed. "And you boil it in a huge caldron over a roaring fire and dance around it at midnight, right?"

"Exactly," Danny said. "Are you going to be home later tonight, say around 7:00? I can come by with the stuff and show you how to apply it too."

"That'd be great. I'll have the coffee on—or maybe fresh lemonade?"

"Either is fine with me, Julie. See you then."

As Julie drove her new Dodge pickup truck out of the *News-Express* parking lot later that afternoon, some of the euphoria she'd been experiencing because of her new assignment began drifting away. She had no doubt that she could handle the weekly pieces—and handle them well—but the responsibility that had fallen to her began to sink in. As she drove to the end of Main Street, her eyes lingered on the boarded-up shops and stores, their plywood-sheeted windows and doors reminding her of photographs she'd seen in a *National Geographic* series on the effects of the Oklahoma

Dust Bowl and the Great Depression. Coldwater was a tidy, well-maintained town, but the brooding, empty stores gave the street an aura of shabbiness and defeat. Very few pedestrians walked the sidewalks, but Julie figured that was due more to the stultifying heat than to economic conditions. Most folks did their shopping in the evening now, when the temperature would generally drop a few blessed degrees.

Julie reached down to adjust her radio as she approached the Bulldogger, the bar Nancy had mentioned. The parking lot was almost filled with pickups and cars, and the front door was open, releasing a thick cloud of tobacco smoke into the still air. Even over the sound of her own radio, the raucous blaring of country rock from the bar throbbed in her ears, the bass line pounding like a massive drum.

Almost before she knew what was happening, a rusted and battered old Ford pickup blasted from the parking lot, banged heavily over the curb, and slewed directly into Julie's path, its body leaning far to one side on ineffective shocks and springs as the driver attempted to wrestle the truck into control. Julie jammed on her brakes and hauled the steering wheel to her right instinctively, away from the truck that was sliding toward her sideways.

The unmuffled roar of the old Ford became the only sound in Julie's universe as her Dodge skidded to the side of the road. The impact of her front wheels slamming over the curb threw her forward sharply into the embrace of her shoulder harness.

Julie got a quick look at the driver of the out-of-control truck as he fought to straighten it in the road. He was young,

21

tanned, with longish hair that swept well over his collar from under the dark Stetson he wore. Amazingly, he was grinning as he battled his vehicle—perhaps even laughing. The back end of the Ford skidded past the left front of Julie's stalled truck, tires spinning hard and putting clouds of acrid smoke into the air. Then it was gone, racing away from Julie as quickly as it had come on her, until even the racket of its engine disappeared.

Several men had come out of the Bulldogger and stood near the door for a few moments, looking across and down Main Street at Julie's truck. Julie turned away from them, away from their laughter and the remarks she was glad she couldn't hear. She shifted into reverse and eased her front end back over the curb and onto the road.

After a mile she was breathing normally and her hands had stopped their almost spastic dance on the steering wheel. Her truck tracked properly, with no pull to either side. There was no increase in exhaust sound; the high clearance of the Dodge had saved her muffler and catalytic converter when she went over the curb. She dragged the back of a hand across her eyes.

What if there had been another car coming? What if that drunken jerk had crashed into a station wagon with a mom and a bunch of kids in it? What if . . .

By the time Julie turned into her driveway and pulled her truck next to her three-stall barn, the adrenaline rush that had swung her startled fear into hot anger had receded. She was sweaty, tired, and weary of the sun that seemed to launch itself at her as she stepped out of her truck.

She took a deep breath and looked around her home. The old house—an eighty-year-old two bedroom—was the only bright spot on her forty acres. Freshly painted a year ago, its white was pristine and sharp, and the black shutters were stark and shiny against the purity of the expanse of white. Her barn would be a project for next year's vacation. It needed paint and some minor repairs, but it stood straight and true and made Julie proud as she looked at it.

The rest of her ranch seemed to be composed of shades of an arid, dusty brown. Her main pasture—almost thirty fenced acres—reflected waves of heat back toward the almost impossibly deep blue of the sky. The grass, in previous years lush and rich with nutrition, looked as if it had been purposely burned over. There'd been no measurable rain for over a year, and the temperature had hovered well above its average since winter ended. There'd been no real spring. August heat had begun in late April and hadn't released its death grip on that part of Montana since then.

The sparse handful of pines that stood baking near Julie's far fence line looked as if they'd given up the battle with the drought—their limbs were tainted a dull brown and were sagging slightly, looking ready to die. Julie's eyes went to her lawn. All cosmetic sprinkling, car washing, and swimming pool filling had been restricted for several months. The allegedly hardy grass seed Julie had painstakingly worked into the ground in the front and sides of her home had withered and died. Very few of the bulbs she'd planted around her foundation had germinated, and those that had were strangled by the sun within days.

23

As she approached the barn her eyes focused on a white paper bag resting under the handle of the sliding door. She bent to pick it up, seeing the name "The Coldwater Apothecary" printed on it. She opened it. Two Snickers bars peeked back at her. The boy in the truck, the heat, the new assignment, even the drought left her mind immediately as she gazed at the melting candy bars. She experienced a sparklike sensation, and then she laughed.

Julie shoved the large front door of the barn open a couple of feet on its roller track and stepped inside, letting her eyes acclimate to the semi-darkness in the center aisle. She placed the paper bag on a shelf to the side. The barn smelled wonderful, as it always did. The scent of the good, tightly baled hay stacked on the second floor was as sweet as the smell of a dewy morning, and the odor of well-cared-for leather and the creosote wood preservative created what was called "cowboy's perfume," a delight to the sense of any horse lover.

Drifter, in the end stall, snorted noisily and stamped a front hoof to get Julie moving to him with his usual snack of a carrot or a small crab apple. When Julie took an extra moment to let the peace of her barn soothe her, Drifter snorted again, this time louder and more demandingly. "Oh, hush," Julie laughed, but she hurried to the gelding's stall and picked up an apple from a basket on a shelf as she walked by. "Here ya go," she said as she extended the treat on the flat of her palm over the top board of the stall.

Drifter lipped the apple from Julie's hand, leaving in its place a viscous mix of saliva and bits of chewed hay. Years of habit caused her to wipe her hand on the back of her pants—before she remembered she was wearing work slacks rather than jeans. A piece of cloth dipped into Drifter's water pail did a fine job of spreading the mess over Julie's pocket as she scrubbed at it. She sighed and tossed the cloth aside as she looked in on her horse.

Drifter was a pretty boy, and he knew it. He was proud to the point of arrogance, in the way only a vibrantly healthy and powerful horse can be. He was buckskin—a color of the Quarter Horse breed that was like a rich, buttery caramel—with a distinctive dorsal stripe that ran the length of his spine in a deeper, almost mahogany hue. He was a full 16 hands tall—a hand being four inches in horseman's jargon—and weighed about 1,150 pounds. His eyes, a liquid brown deep enough to fall into, were alert, intelligent, and endlessly curious.

Drifter was, beyond any doubt, the fastest, smartest, and generally the best horse Julie had ever owned.

She led him out of his stall and cross-tied him in the central aisle. The marks that had concerned her were low on the backs of his legs, in the area a couple of inches from the ground. The tissue there, generally tight and hairy, looked damp and abraded, as if the flesh had been partially scuffed away. The flesh had a slightly acidic smell, and it glistened in the overhead light Julie had snapped on. She left Drifter standing in the cross ties and fetched a few cotton balls from her supply cabinet. She crouched next to the horse and very gently touched cotton to where the seeping seemed to originate. Drifter tensed and attempted to shift away from Julie.

She stood, stroked his neck until he calmed, and led him back into his stall. *Danny will tell me exactly what to do,* she thought. *I could make things worse by playing veterinarian.*

She fetched another crab apple for Drifter and palmed it to him. He chewed happily, grunting slightly with pleasure as he did so. Julie checked the level of water in his pail and then headed for her house, thinking of the faith and trust she had in Dan Pulver, DVM.

She and Danny shared a lot of similarities. They were close in age; Danny was thirty-seven, a year older than Julie. Both loved small-town living. Neither had ever been married. They both attended Coldwater Church and were active in study groups and worship meetings. Maggie Lane, wife of minister Ian Lane, in fact, was Julie's most cherished female friend. Danny and Ian were good friends too, although it was no secret that the vet had been in love with Maggie before she and Ian were married. That, however, had been a couple of years ago.

Danny and Julie had gone out a few times. Once, they'd attended the Montana Barrel Racing Finals at the Coldwater Arena. It had been a fun and laughter-filled day, and Julie had been certain Danny would call her the following week. He hadn't. Another time they'd spent an afternoon riding together, Danny on his gentle Appaloosa and Julie on Drifter. That too had been a great day. They'd talked easily and, at least in Julie's mind, had enjoyed their time together. Again, though, Danny hadn't called to follow up on the good day. Apparently he wasn't interested in seeing what could possibly develop between them if they spent more time together.

Julie sighed as she opened the door and stepped into her kitchen. Her home didn't seem to welcome her as it always had in the years she'd owned it. Instead, the contained heat weighed her down and made the smallest household tasks into major expenditures of energy that simply didn't seem worth the trouble. Her cereal bowl and juice glass sat in the sink, and a sheaf of mail—mostly bills, circulars, and advertising—was strewn across the kitchen table. A carton of milk stood on the shelf near the refrigerator; she had obviously forgotten to put it back in the fridge that morning. Julie picked it up, the soft warmth of the plastic an unpleasant sensation in her hand. She screwed off the top, dumped the contents into the sink, and ran some water. The foul odor of curdled milk was repulsive enough to cause hot bile to rise in the back of her throat. Then, halfheartedly, she washed and rinsed her breakfast dishes, realizing that if it hadn't been for Danny coming by that evening, she wouldn't have bothered.

This is part of the drought, she thought. *This is what the ceaseless heat can do to the psyche. And this feeling would only be magnified if my cattle were dropping weight because of burned pastures, or if I were depending on the profits of a failed few hundred acres of wheat or corn or hay to get me through the winter. Suppose I were feeding horses I'd raised and trained to sell and there were no buyers—even at steeply reduced prices—and hay and feed bills were piling up, unpaid?*

"That's where the stories are," she said aloud. "Those sorts of things are what I need to go after." Her voice sounded hollow in the empty house—hollow and a bit lonely. "A shower," she said, forcing some anticipation into her voice, even though she was the only one hearing it. "That'll straighten out the world, the drought, the heat, and me!"

She tossed her Drifter-soiled slacks into the corner of her bedroom and put her blouse on a hanger, hoping to get another day out of it later on in the week. In a beat-up and faded bathrobe she'd had for more years than she cared to remember, she padded barefoot down the hall to her bathroom. Her Mickey Mouse shower curtain brought a smile to her face, as it always did. Mickey stood in a starburst of brilliant white, clutching a pen in one three-fingered hand and a spiral pad in the other. The caption beneath him read "Writers is good peopple." Julie swept Mickey and his sentiments to the side and cranked on the hot water.

The metallic cough from the showerhead rattled the pipes from the basement to the second floor. Julie's well was a good one—deep, with sweet water that had never failed her. For a long moment, nothing happened. Then, the pipes clattered again, louder and more violently this time, as if some lunatic were shaking them, and the shower expelled another burst of air. Julie stood at the side of the tub, her hands grasped into fists, and whispered a quick prayer. *Please, Lord—not my well.*

When water gushed forth from the showerhead, Julie released the tension in her hands and let her shoulders sag in relief. The bulletins she'd collected from the State of Montana Water Conservation Service had warned her and all the others in her part of the state about the frighteningly low status of the water table, and how well problems were not only possible but expected. The thumping pressure of the flow against her hand was a precious gift, and perhaps for the first time she realized that.

A quick image of the Coldwater Suds-Spot, the local laundromat, flicked into her mind. She'd wondered in an abstract sort of way why so many cars and pickups were parked in the place's lot every day. Now, she realized the answer: every bit of water used for laundry was that much less for the crops, cattle, and horses on the farms and ranches. Folks paid to wash their clothes rather than deplete their own wells.

Julie rinsed her hair and let the water wash the suds from her body and then turned off the handles without the final deluge she so enjoyed standing under. Her mental picture of the Suds-Spot made her feel wasteful of an invaluable commodity—and she didn't like that sensation at all.

In her robe and bare feet she settled in at the small desk in her tiny home office, hair still damp and a towel over her shoulders. Nancy's releasing her from her column was fine, but it had no effect on the stories and pieces Julie had begun to research or had already started to write. *The drought series isn't going to last forever,* she told herself. She pulled a file folder from her drawer and clicked on her computer. While the system booted up, she paged through her scrawled notes on an interview she'd done with a state legislator concerning a piece of legislation that could alter the grazing rights of ranchers on state lands. The crux of the article was there in front of her, seeming to hide from her in her notes. *C'mon, Julie,* she chided herself. *This is awfully important to the cattle people.* She pecked out a few words—a tentative lead. That led to a full paragraph, and another paragraph . . .

She was startled when she looked away from her monitor to the face of the old Westclock windup alarm clock she kept on her desk. She scurried to her bedroom to dress.

Danny pulled in at about five minutes after 7:00, his GMC truck trailing a cloud of thick dust behind him. Julie watched from her kitchen window as he climbed out of his vehicle and then reached back inside for a blue glass jar about the size of a container of economy-sized Vicks VapoRub. He arched his back for a moment, stretching, and then snapped his fingers. His collie, Sunday, leaped out of the truck and stood next to Danny, looking up at him, his plumed tail wagging slowly, questioningly, as he watched Danny's face.

Julie smiled. A couple of generations ago, women would have referred to Dr. Pulver as a dreamboat. He was an inch or so over six feet tall, lean, with somewhat scruffy, over-the-collar sandy brown hair. His facial features were angular, but his mouth was generous and his eyes a fathomless chestnut. He looked not unlike a young Paul Newman, and he moved with a certain fluidity and lack of self-consciousness that clearly stated he had no idea what a stunning effect he had on women.

Through some hand motion Julie didn't catch, or perhaps

by a word she couldn't hear, Danny had brought his dog leaping into heel position from the passenger seat.

Julie shoved open the kitchen door. "Hey, Danny—thanks for stopping by."

Julie took a deep breath when Danny smiled at her with genuine warmth.

"Glad to be here, Julie—I've been looking forward to visiting with you."

"I've been looking forward to seeing you too," Julie said, her smile every bit as welcoming as his.

"Last call of the day," he went on. "Boy, it feels good."

Julie swallowed hard. "C'mon in and have a cup of coffee."

Danny stopped a couple of steps from the door Julie was holding open. "OK if Sunday wanders a bit?"

Julie had never come across a dog quite like Danny Pulver's collie. It seemed like every family in Coldwater had at least one well-trained dog, but Sunday went far beyond being well trained. Julie had no more problem with him exploring around her home and barn than she would have with a well-behaved child.

"Sure. And I just might have a Milk-Bone with his name on it when we go back out." She opened the door a bit wider, and Danny walked into her kitchen.

2

Julie poured Danny some coffee from the fresh pot on the stove. Danny sipped appreciatively, waving away the offer of milk and sugar. "Whew—that's good. It's been a long day."

"Lots of appointments?"

"Yeah. I feel like I'm aboard Noah's ark. I've treated cows, pigs, horses, a bird, and three cats today."

"Business must be good, then."

Danny's smile disappeared. "In a sense it is—and in another sense, it's terrible. So many of my clients simply don't have . . ." He stopped himself and looked guiltily at Julie. "I shouldn't . . ."

"Don't have the money to pay for your services," Julie finished for him.

Danny nodded. "Well, yeah. This drought—the price of feed and hay, the almost nonexistent crops—people are right against the wall. The thing is, if I don't get paid, I can't keep up with my payments for supplies, medication, equipment, all the stuff I need to run my practice." He sighed. "Sorry about the whining. Let's change the subject. What's new with you?"

"It's not whining, Danny. Not at all. The local economy is in tough shape, and some ranchers and farmers are barely hanging on. If the drought doesn't break soon, there's going to be For Sale signs sprouting like weeds around Coldwater."

Danny nodded and held out his cup to Julie. "Can I get a refill?" He grinned like a boy requesting another piece of pie, and Julie returned the smile.

"You bet," she said, standing and stepping to the stove. "One good thing did happen to me today—even beyond you diagnosing what's wrong with Drifter. Nancy Lewis called me into her office this morning and gave me the biggest assignment I've ever had."

"Great! Tell me about it."

Julie told him about the meeting, and he listened carefully, his eyes locked with hers, as if she were telling him the most important information he'd ever heard. Finally, becoming a bit embarrassed about rattling on so long about herself, Julie ended with a lame, "That's about it."

"I'm really impressed," Danny said. "I know your column is doing well and that folks talk about what you write. This drought series can do a whole bunch of good. While you were explaining what you're going to do, FDR's line came to my mind: 'Nothing to fear but fear itself.' Natural things like droughts always end, and things always get better. If we can keep in mind that this'll pass, maybe try to help our neighbors in any way we can, we'll get through it."

"I believe that too, Danny. But it's easy for me to say. I haven't really been hurt much."

Danny finished his coffee. "One thing none of us—from the richest to the poorest—have escaped is the heat. It's the great leveler. I've never experienced anything like it." He shook his head. "I came across a word in a book yesterday that I didn't recognize, so I looked it up. *Enervate*—it means a loss of strength and vigor, a kind of sapping of life power. It seems like that's what the heat is doing—draining away the spirit of the land and the crops and even the people."

"It does seem like that at times," Julie said. "I've heard about men getting drunk and fighting at the Bulldogger, guys who'd been friends for years or at least had known each other for years."

"I've heard," Danny said. "Isn't the town council trying to shut the place down?"

"No legal grounds yet, I guess," Julie said.

Danny took a breath and stood, reaching for the blue glass jar he'd set on the counter as he came in. "Let's go take a look at Drifter, OK?" Then he added, "Have you heard about the Kendricks kid? Dean?"

"I know the name. He works on the Nowack farm, right? Was on the rodeo circuit a bit last summer?"

"Yeah, that's him. He was a pretty good roper. Made some rides on saddle broncs too. Old Man Nowack laid him off a couple of weeks ago. No crops, no work. Anyway, Dean got drunk somewhere this afternoon and drove that junk heap of a truck of his into a tree. He broke a leg and several ribs, and both his wrists. Had a severe concussion too."

35

Julie's hand came to her mouth, and she began to feel dizzy. "Is he going to make it?"

"I don't . . . Julie! What's wrong?" He rushed to her and eased her down into the chair she'd just stood from, his hands clutching her shoulders to keep her upright.

Julie reached up and put her hand on Danny's wrist. The strength of it felt very good. "I . . . I just need a second. I got a little dizzy, is all." She slumped back a bit, and Danny's hand on her shoulder tightened. She let her head drop forward so that her chin rested on her chest. "Just give me a minute. I'll be OK."

"Sure. I'm right here. I won't let you fall. You're OK. Take some deep breaths as soon as you can. It's the heat . . ."

Within a pair of minutes she felt the color return to her face. "Danny," she began, but her voice cracked. "Danny, do you know what kind of truck the Kendricks boy had?"

"Sure. It's a rust-bucket Ford with no muffler and no working lights. I gave him a jump last winter. Why do you want to know?"

Julie took a breath. "A guy in an old Ford came skidding out of the parking lot at the Bulldogger this afternoon and almost slammed into me. He was laughing, like it was a joke or something. He was all over the road, and then he got control and turned down a side street, going real fast."

"Dean Kendricks?" Danny asked.

Julie shook her head. "I don't know. It could've been."

"If he was driving around loaded, it's a wonder he didn't hurt or kill someone. That's pretty scary."

Julie shook her head again. "What's scary is that I did

36

nothing. I should've called the police right away. I had my cell phone, and I could describe the truck and the driver. I could've prevented what happened to him—and I didn't. I didn't do anything. I sat there for a few minutes, shaky and scared, and then I drove home."

Danny put a hand on her arm. "You had absolutely no way of knowing what was going to happen, Julie. You said his truck almost hit yours. You were scared and not thinking straight. Who would be in that situation? Don't beat yourself up over this."

Julie forced a smile. "I'd like a glass of water, please," she said.

Danny fetched the water and hovered at her side until she was done drinking.

"Just give me a minute, and then we can go out to the barn, OK?"

Danny moved reluctantly to the chair closest to her.

Julie closed her eyes for a moment. The truck sliding toward her immediately appeared in stunning color and detail, followed by a fuzzy, indistinct image of the same truck slamming into a tree.

She opened her eyes. "How old is Dean Kendricks?" she asked.

"How old is he?" Danny thought for a moment. "Nineteen—maybe twenty at the outside. He graduated high school last year."

Julie nodded. "Let's go fix ol' Drifter, Doc."

Sunday was stretched out next to Danny's truck and started to rise when Danny and Julie stepped out of the

37

house. "Good boy," Danny murmured and gave a hand signal indicating "stay." The collie settled back down, following the couple with his eyes.

Drifter stood easily in the cross ties, gnawing on a large carrot. Danny and Julie crouched shoulder to shoulder facing the inside of the geldings' front legs; Danny held the uncapped jar of medication. "Just take a glop of this on a finger," he said, doing exactly that, "and rub it in over the abrasions. Don't press too hard, and make sure you spread it around well. Here—try it." He held out the jar to Julie.

She sniffed it. "Smells a little minty," she said.

"There's some mentholatum in there—and pine tar and udder balm and petroleum jelly and an antibiotic—"

"And the eye of newt, of course," Julie added.

"And spunk water from a cemetery, like in *Tom Sawyer*," Danny said.

Julie laughed and lost her balance for a moment as she took the jar from Danny's hand. Their foreheads knocked together, and her nose nudged his. They separated quickly, red faced.

They both began to speak at once—and both stopped at once. Danny lifted his hand and touched Julie's hair very gently with his fingertips. Julie exhaled lightly and closed her eyes.

And then, as quickly as it had begun, the moment was over. Drifter snorted, seeking another treat, and Julie and Danny stood up, self-consciously moving apart a couple of steps.

"Do that twice a day, morning and evening," he said in his veterinarian's voice.

"When should I see an improvement? Can I use him?"

"Sure. There's no disability involved. He's fine. Use up the salve and then give me a call, and I'll stop by to see how things look."

Danny stood to one side as Julie unclipped the cross ties and led Drifter back to his stall. She secured the stall door, gave the horse another carrot, and walked with Danny to the front of the barn. Danny snapped his fingers lightly, and Sunday trotted over, tail swinging.

"He's a great dog," Julie said.

"He's the best," Danny agreed proudly. He glanced at his watch. "I'd better get on the road. Early appointment tomorrow to look at that gored cow again—change the dressings, check for infection. Oh—that reminds me. Do you like good beef? Jimmy gave me a couple of prime steaks about the size of saddle blankets."

"Sure! We could grill—"

"Just a sec," Danny said. He opened the sliding door of his truck and flipped the top off an Igloo cooler. He took out a two-pound steak wrapped in brown paper and handed it to Julie. "I hope you enjoy it." Danny smiled at her and then motioned Sunday into the truck, shut the door, and moved to the front of the vehicle.

"Call if there are any problems with Drifter—but there won't be."

"Let me get a check . . ."

"I'll send an invoice," he said, starting his engine. "G'night, Julie—nice visiting with you."

Julie stood and watched Danny's taillights recede down the driveway. The steak felt heavy in her hands. She looked down at it for a long moment. Then she laughed. The situation was so ludicrous that there was absolutely nothing else she could have done.

And she'd completely forgotten Sunday's Milk-Bone.

Julie's sleep was fitful that night, just as it had been most nights since the extreme temperatures had invaded her part of the state. Air-conditioning was a wonderful option, but most of the ranches and homes weren't wired for the sort of power that central units required, and the window models didn't have the cooling power to fight the high nineties. As a consequence, although most of the stores and public buildings were air-conditioned, only a few ranchers or farm families could afford the luxury—particularly now.

The next morning Julie watched Drifter head across the pasture to where the pines stood, his hooves raising ugly little puffs of grit where pasture grass should have been growing. She went back into the barn and mucked out Drifter's stall. She spread a light coating of lime on the floor, sifting it like flour through her fingers. By the time she'd replaced the wet and soiled straw and tossed a thick flake of hay into the corner of the stall, she was drenched in sweat. The air—even at barely 5:30 a.m.—was thick and motionless and heavy, seeming to blanket the usual sweet smells of the barn.

The idea had come to her while Danny was still there the night before, during their talk in the kitchen. It was a germ of a concept at that time, but the hours of twisting and turning in bed had given Julie more than enough time to allow it to grow into what could be the first of her drought series articles.

Danny Pulver had taken over some of Julie's time that night too.

What is with that guy? Is he afraid of me for some reason? Am I coming on too strong? Or is there someone else in his life?

Julie found herself standing outside Drifter's stall, staring at the wall, her hay fork slung over her shoulder. She shook her head.

So what, then? He doesn't much care for me. Big deal. He's just another guy. Who needs him? Ken Townsend certainly seemed interested in me, even if Danny doesn't. The thought of the pair of Snickers bars in the paper sack brought a smile to Julie's face, despite the heat. *OK—so I know next to nothing about Ken. But he seems like a good man. Maybe I'll get a chance to find that out if he follows through and calls me.*

Julie shook her head again, refusing to follow the thought. Still, she couldn't help but think about Danny again. He had been an enigma ever since she'd met him. There was something about the man—a sort of innocence maybe—that touched her heart in a way she hadn't experienced before. And she couldn't help but think that the attraction was mutual. But if it were, why didn't he act on it?

A few minutes later, after she had finished mucking the stall and headed for the bathroom, the showerhead coughed and gasped and the pipes rattled as if they were trying to escape from their confines behind lathe and plaster and multiple coats of paint. But the water ultimately came. Her shower was quick—hurried and not particularly satisfying. The specter of failing water supplies was close to Julie's consciousness.

She dried and dressed, selecting jeans and a button-down collar shirt and, of course, her boots. After eating a quick breakfast, she got in her truck and drove slowly to Coldwater, more than a little nervous—and maybe a bit afraid. She wrote a headline in her mind and then laughed at it:

Intrepid Reporter Lost in Den of Iniquity!

A couple of pickups and three cars were in the parking lot of the Bulldogger when Julie pulled in and eased to a stop near the front door. She checked her watch: 7:27 a.m. The beer light advertisements in the windows weren't on yet, she noticed, but she heard conversation from inside. She got out of her truck, locked the door, and took a deep breath. Then she opened the door.

The lighting in the Bulldogger was murky, maybe because the air was already fouled with thick clouds of cigarette and cigar smoke. Or maybe because most of the overhead fluorescents either flickered weakly or were completely dead. While Julie squinted, trying to adjust her eyes, the four men seated at the bar turned to look at her.

The one closest to her, a heavyset fellow with several empty beer bottles in front of him, turned on his stool.

42

Julie thought it had to have been at least a couple of days since he'd shaved. He wore a black leather vest over a gray T-shirt, and his jeans and boots were worn and dusty. He held a cigarette between the first two fingers of his right hand, and the smoke from it curled up toward the darkness of the ceiling.

"Ya lost?" he asked.

Julie swallowed hard. "No. I'm not. I'm looking for Rick Castle." She was proud of her voice—both its tone and the message it carried. "Is he around?"

The heavy man stared at her and took a long drag on his cigarette but didn't answer.

The bartender, a man not terribly different in looks from the one who'd spoken to Julie, said, "We ain't open yet, honey. You come on back at 8:00, and I'll take good care of you."

"I asked if Rick Castle was around," Julie said. "How about an answer? And if you're not open, what're you doing serving these guys?"

A voice called out from the end of the bar, where there was almost no light at all. "Those fellas are employees, lady. There's no law against an employee havin' a beer before we open."

Julie stared back into the darkness, seeing only a tall figure.

"I'm Castle. What do you want?"

"I'm Julie Downs—*News-Express*. I want to talk with you."

"Well, what if I don't want to talk to you?"

"Then maybe I'll just go talk with the Montana Liquor

43

Board and the Coldwater town council and to the parents of the minor you overserved yesterday until he got so drunk he almost killed himself trying to find his way home." She waited for a beat. "You ever hear of the Dram Shop Acts, Mr. Castle? The law that says an owner of a place like this is liable and responsible for what happens to the people he serves to the point of obvious intoxication?"

"You got nothin'. Nothin' at all. I suggest you get lost."

"Do you really want to bet on that, Mr. Castle? Remember when Dean Kendricks left here yesterday? How he almost crashed into a nice, new Dodge truck? I was driving the Dodge."

"That punk wasn't here yesterday or any other day. I don't serve minors, an' neither do my bartenders. Like I said, get lost."

"Sure," Julie said agreeably. "But Mr. Castle—film doesn't lie, does it? My cameraman is awfully good—don't you think he could take pictures of a kid almost falling into his vehicle as he leaves this place and then bucking over the curb onto Main Street—"

"I don't believe you. You got no tape."

"Thanks for your time and your hospitality, Mr. Castle," Julie said. She turned and started toward the door. *I blew it,* she thought. *I pushed too hard. I shouldn't have tacked on that videotape bit.*

The moment her hand touched the doorknob, Castle's voice called out, "Wait a minute. Come on back. We can talk in my office."

Julie sighed silently and stifled a grin. "Put some lights on back there."

A couple of fluorescent tubes begrudgingly flickered on. Julie started down the length of the bar, the soles of her boots sticking to beer and booze. The eyes on her back as she walked caused a palpable sensation—as if she were being spat upon.

Castle was a man of about fifty; he wore a wristwatch that appeared to be a Rolex until Julie looked at it more closely, and a tangle of gold chains around his neck. He was tall, rather lean, with neatly combed short hair that didn't look quite natural. When he opened a door and turned on the light inside a storage room/office, Julie saw he was wearing a toupee—and an apparently inexpensive one at that.

"Sit," Castle said, pointing to a folding chair. He moved behind a gray metal desk and sat on another folding chair. Cases of whiskey and cartons of potato chips and pretzels were stacked against the walls in the small and hideously hot room. Huge jugs of maraschino cherries rested on top of an obviously defunct air-conditioning unit. The place smelled like the primate cage of a zoo.

Julie sat and locked eyes with Castle.

"So, what's your beef?" he said. "I run a clean business here."

"I'm not at all certain that's true. A kid—a boy who was too young for you to serve—left this place and—"

"We check IDs. No kids get served in here."

"And almost killed himself. Since the drought got severe you've been opening earlier, right?"

"No law against that," Castle said. "Men are outta work. It's good for them to have a place to go be with their pals."

Julie snorted. "And to get drunk and fight and spend what little money they have—and maybe kill themselves or someone else on the way home?"

"I don't know what you're talkin' about, and it ain't my problem how these yahoos spend their time or money. Look—I got work to do. What's your point?"

"This: I wanted to talk to you before I wrote my story about this place and the damage it's doing to the community. I wanted to hear your side. I've done that. Thanks for your time, Mr. Castle." Julie stood and opened the door.

Castle smirked. "Don't ever play poker with a man, lady. You don't have that tape you made up no more than I have the Hope Diamond."

Julie didn't respond. Walking the length of the bar was, once again, like walking a gauntlet. This time, however, Julie was facing the men on stools, and her eyes met with those of each man. Two of them looked away, almost sheepishly, and focused on their drinks. None of them said a word.

The air outside the Bulldogger was steamy and smelled of melting asphalt and the acrid exhaust fumes of a diesel rig that had just lumbered by—and to Julie Downs, at least for a few moments, it was as sweet and pure as a cool spring morning after what she'd breathed inside the bar.

She stepped to the passenger side of her truck, unlocked the door, and took her Nikon from the glove compartment. She walked across the parking lot, avoiding shards of broken glass and puddles of oil from leaking engines.

The road told the story as clearly as any words could. Kendricks's tracks began in the lot, where his spinning tires and his sideways momentum had dug through the stones and debris to the dirt beneath, jumped the curb, and skidded out into the street. Julie's skid lines were much darker, parallel black streaks gouged into the surface of the road, and showed how she'd swerved to avoid impact, banged over the curb, and stopped. She took eight or ten shots of the roadway. As she walked back to her truck she saw Rick Castle standing in front of the door of the Bulldogger. He spat to one side and raised his arm in an obscene gesture, and Julie raised her camera at the same time.

"Gotcha," she said to herself.

Drago's Café on Main Street in Coldwater had served the town and the county as an unofficial meeting place for almost thirty years. Regulars met for breakfast every day but Sunday, the lunch crowd was always large, and countless high school romances had begun—and ended—within its walls. The food was good, the coffee was strong and hot and never more than a few minutes old, and the ambiance was comfortable and easy. Referred to as "the diner" by most of the cowhands, the café drew people at all times of day who were seeking a hit of caffeine, a piece of pie, or some conversation.

It was too early for the pie, but the coffee and conversation sounded just fine to Julie. She parked next to a familiar Chevrolet pickup with a Montana Barrel Racing Association sticker on its rear window and hustled through the heat to the café.

Maggie Lane, wife of Rev. Ian Lanc, was Julie's best friend and had been so for several years. Before marrying Ian, Maggie had operated her Quarter Horse breeding and training facility alone after the death of her first husband. Now she and Ian shared both ranch and church duties. Julie called out to her friend, who was sitting at the counter, a cup of coffee and a large pastry on a plate in front of her. Maggie smiled and patted the empty stool next to her. "Hey, Julie—sit down." She pointed at the pastry. "Get fat with me."

"Fat?" Julie said as she sat down. "You could eat a truckload of anvils and not gain an ounce. Ian with you?"

Maggie shook her head. "No, he's sleeping, actually. He was at the hospital all night with the family of a kid who'd been in a car wreck." Maggie must have noticed the change in Julie's face immediately. "What's the matter?"

"Dean Kendricks, right?" Julie asked quietly.

Maggie nodded. "You know him?"

An older fellow in working cowhand clothes stopped next to Maggie, clutching his Stetson in his large hands. "Uh . . . Maggie? I saw Rev. Lane last night at the hospital with Dean's folks. They—all of us—were sure glad he was there, ma'am."

"I'll tell him you mentioned it, Jake. Thanks. Julie and I were just talking—"

The toe of Julie's boot found the side of Maggie's foot quickly and painfully.

"Uh, talking about . . . the heat," Maggie finished some-what lamely.

The cowhand nodded to Julie. "It's a sad thing," Jake went on. "That scrapheap the kid drove didn't have no more brakes on it than a fresh-broke colt. Dean, he's a good boy. Awful good roper for a kid too. I figured he was gonna take open ropin' over at Dansville come next Sunday. Now . . ." Jake went silent, his eyes heavy and sad. After a moment, he said, "I'd best be on my way." He headed for the front door.

"Let's get a booth," Julie said. "Why don't you grab one and I'll get some coffee?" She walked to the counter to save a waitress the trip.

After she sat down in the booth with her coffee, Julie explained to Maggie about what had happened the day before, where she'd been not half an hour ago, and why she'd been there.

"I'm happy for you about the series, Julie. But I'm not sure I see how the Bulldogger and Dean Kendricks fit into the drought. I know the place is a cesspool and always has been, but how—"

"Don't you see, Maggie?" Julie interrupted. "If you give a roomful of little kids some loaded handguns to play with, somebody's going to get hurt real soon. Correct? Castle running his gin mill more hours acts like a magnet, drawing the men who've been put out of work by the drought. And I've verified that the Kendricks kid is barely twenty years old. He can't legally drink or buy alcohol, but Castle served and overserved him to the point where he was driving like a lunatic."

Maggie remained dubious. "I don't know. Sure, Dean is too young to drink legally, but it seems to me that there are other factors involved. Suppose he had a good fake ID? Lots of kids do. Or suppose the guy who almost crashed into you wasn't Kendricks? See what I mean? It could be a great story and it could even close down that dump for good, but I think you need to tread carefully. That's all."

"I know what I saw. I've got photos of the skid marks from the kid's truck and my own. I saw his face, and I can match it to his high school graduation picture." Julie's voice had risen with the intensity of what she was saying. A couple of heads at the counter turned to look over at the booth.

Julie sighed. "Sorry, Maggie. I didn't mean to take your head off. This thing—this story—is very close to me."

"I know. I don't mean to knock your story. I'm not trying to be adversarial—really I'm not. I just ... well ... I want you to be careful." She smiled. "OK?"

"I know that," Julie said with perhaps a bit more understanding than she was really feeling. She sipped at her coffee. "Danny was out to my place last night."

Maggie raised her eyebrows. "For dinner?"

"I wish. But no, Drifter has some abrasions on his heels."

"Scratches?" Maggie asked.

"How in the world did you know that?" Julie laughed. "Danny had to make ointment for me. There's no commercial stuff available."

"So ... how did it go with Danny?"

Julie expelled a long breath. "He gave me a steak. I auto-

50

matically thought we'd grill it together—and then he was gone."

Maggie shook her head. "I'm not sure what it is with that man," she said. "I do know this—he's interested in you and he cares for you. What keeps him from letting himself get even a little bit close, I can't figure out."

Julie met her friend's eyes. "Are you certain he's over you, Maggie?"

"Absolutely. I guarantee it. I can't say a whole lot more without breaking confidences, but yeah—I'm certain. And I know he cares for you—for all the good that does if he keeps on avoiding getting to know you better."

Although there was barely a half inch of coffee remaining in Julie's cup, for some reason she found it necessary to stir it vigorously and closely watch the process—if only to avoid Maggie's eyes. "I get the feeling he's somehow afraid of me," she said quietly.

"Julie . . ."

"No, I mean it. Remember the time Danny and I went riding? We tied our horses and walked a little, and he took my hand, and it felt so natural and good and sweet—and in about a minute he dropped it like I'd burned him or something. I asked him what the matter was, and he got all red faced and backed away and said he had to check the horses."

"OK," Maggie said. "What about later?"

"We rode some more and then went back, and I tried to ask him about it again, but he clammed up in that exasperating way he has."

"Well," Maggie said, "I don't understand it either. Danny Pulver is a tough one to figure out." She checked her watch. "Oh, shoot. I have to run. Ian's doing a mailing, and I need to pick up a ton of stamps." She paused for a moment. "Are we OK about your story, Julie? You're the last person in the world I'd want to hurt, particularly by running my mouth about something I know nothing about."

Julie's smile was real. "We're fine."

Maggie stood. "Good luck with Danny," she whispered.

"Luck? I'll need more than that," Julie said ruefully.

Maggie patted her friend on the shoulder. "Give me a call tomorrow, OK?"

After Maggie left, Julie motioned one of the Drago kids—Bonnie—to the booth to request another cup of coffee.

"How've you been, Julie?" the girl asked. "I love your column, ya know. It's so not phony like the ones in the big papers." She stretched the word *so* until it almost collapsed.

"I've been fine, Bonnie. I'm glad you like my column."

The girl smiled and began to turn away.

"Bonnie," Julie said, stopping her, "do you know Dean Kendricks?"

"Sure. He just graduated last year. Cool guy. Isn't it awful about his accident?"

"Terrible." She waited a heartbeat. "What kind of a kid is he?"

Bonnie didn't need to stop and think. "Fun—funny. Not a rocket scientist, but his grades are OK. He hangs with the kids on the rodeo team most of the time. Not a stoner or anything. Horse crazy. Heck of a roper. Cute too."

"Mmm," Julie nodded. "Thanks."

Julie sipped at her cup of coffee while her mind replayed her conversation with Maggie. *Is the story too much for the News-Express? Am I pushing too hard because of my feelings about alcohol and the accident I almost had with that poor kid? Would anything really change if the Bulldogger were closed down? The drought is the drought, and until it's over, can a bunch of words in a small newspaper—a series of articles— accomplish anything?*

Julie answered her own question with a whisper. "Yeah. It can. It will."

But then another self-chiding headline formed in her mind, unbidden as usual, in stark, bold letters:

Plucky Reporter Changes World, Ends Drought
Everything on Earth Perfect Because of Series

Julie smiled in spite of herself. Her "headlines" had started out as a sort of game between her and her roommate at journalism school when they began leaving notes for one another taped to the bathroom mirror or on each other's desks: "Date Flops—David Found to Be Geek," "Pop Quiz Ends Journalism Career," and "Roommate Indicted on Messiness Charges." Somehow, the silly headlines had become part of Julie, and they popped up in her mind seemingly of their own volition.

Julie finished her coffee but didn't get up from the booth. *I need to get over Danny Pulver,* she thought. *I'm like a teenager infatuated with the captain of the high school football team. I've given the guy chances—maybe too many—to see if there can be something between us. Enough is enough. Danny no longer possesses any space in my mind.*

As she slid out of the booth, she found herself almost nose to nose with Ken Townsend.

"Oh!" Julie peeped.

"Please don't hurt me," Ken said in a feminine voice.

"Ken—I was kind of . . ."

"Lost in space?" he asked.

"Exactly."

"I saw your truck outside, and even though I was on my way to solve the crime of the century, I thought I'd pull in and buy you a cup of coffee." He looked into her eyes. "You're under no obligation, of course. Seems to me, though, that press-police relations are the very bedrock of a safe community. And," he added, "I know the secret of the Snickers—"

Julie laughed. "Hush about that! Actually, I'm drowning in coffee. How about I let you buy me a small dish of ice cream?"

"Deal," Ken said, sitting on one side of the booth. Julie settled back across the table from him. "What kind of ice cream?" he asked.

Bonnie, the young waitress, hustled over to the booth, pencil poised over pad.

"A small dish of chocolate," Julie said. "And I mean *small*, Bonnie."

"Sure." The girl smiled. "What about you, Officer?"

"Just coffee for me, thanks, Bonnie. That sundae you made for me last week was dynamite, but it's a little early for—"

A crackle came from the small radio receiver on his belt. He pulled the receiver from its rectangular leather holster and held it to his ear. The smile disappeared from his face as if it'd been slapped away. Ken stood. "I'm really sorry—I need to run. That was the chief. We'll do this again soon, OK?"

Julie watched Ken hustle to the front door. In seconds, she heard the deep roar of his engine.

"Wow," Bonnie said.

"Yeah," Julie said. "My sentiments exactly."

Heat rose in shimmering curtains, like the air above a roaring fire, from the tar surface. Her boots sank into it, reminding her of the grasping, disgusting floor at the Bulldogger. She pawed through her purse for her rarely used press card, found it, and held it in her right hand as she pushed open the door. The cool air that greeted her was almost, but not quite, worth the trek across the parking lot.

Coldwater General wasn't a large hospital. Only four floors in height, it was a boxlike structure with the aesthetic appeal of a chicken coop. Julie knew the physicians and the staff were excellent and that the hospital was highly rated, but even driving by CG released butterflies in her stomach.

The critical care area, she knew, was on the top floor. She strode confidently past the desk and switchboard on the main floor, and no one questioned her. She was the only passenger in the elevator that took her to the CC unit. The doors slid open directly in front of a nursing and reception module, with the rooms spread as spokes around it. The antiseptic smell was stronger here, and the usual hospital background noise seemed subdued, allowing the monotonous but essential-to-life beeps of monitors and other sorts of machines to be the dominant sound.

A nurse seated behind a window looked up at Julie.

"I'm here to see Dean Kendricks," Julie said.

The nurse's eyes opened wider for the briefest part of a second before she recovered her equanimity. "Are you family?" she asked.

"No. Press, actually," Julie said, holding up her card. "I only need a moment—or if I could see Dean's mom or dad, that'd be fine."

The nurse stood. "One moment please," she said and entered an office situated behind her. In a moment she came out, followed by another nurse, an older woman who walked slowly to the window.

"I'm sorry, but Dean Kendricks died of his injuries an hour ago. His family was with him at the end. We've already made the announcement to the *News-Express*."

Julie sat in her truck and paid no attention to the searing temperature around her. Tears streaked her face, and her hands tortured and shredded a tissue she'd gotten from her glove compartment.

"Julie?" She looked up to see Ian Lane standing next to her vehicle. "I guess you heard about the Kendricks boy, right?"

She nodded her head.

"I was just with the family. I saw you leaving the fourth floor and I called to you, but you didn't stop. I caught the next elevator, but it took forever." He paused. "Did you know Dean well?"

Julie shook her head. "I didn't know him at all, but I almost got into an accident with him yesterday. I saw Maggie this morning and told her about it. She'll tell you. OK?"

"Sure. But will you stop by later? Maybe right now isn't the time to talk, but I can see how upset you are. Will you do that? Maggie would love to have you, and so would I."

"I ... I can't, Ian. I'm sorry. I'll be in touch tomorrow, with both of you."

Ian nodded, and when Julie looked at him she saw how drawn and tired his ordinarily open and cheerful face was, how fatigued and reddened his eyes were.

"Tomorrow, then," he said. After a moment, he added, "It's always hard to lose someone. When it's a boy who's barely started his life, it's that much more painful."

Julie couldn't speak. She met the sad eyes of her minister—her friend—again. Then she looked away and started her engine.

The story seemed to cascade from her, at first with the unrestrained power of an opened fire hydrant, but then, later, with the steady flow of a spring stream, constant, strong, but controlled and headed in the right direction.

Her photo layout skills weren't great, but it didn't matter. The *News-Express* staff would take care of all that. The pictures magically appeared from the tiny disk in her camera and then on pages from her printer, and she taped them roughly where she wanted them on her pages.

Julie stopped writing at about midnight, ate a can of cold vegetable soup and an apple, and went back to her office. She'd tended to Drifter when she'd arrived home hours earlier and applied the ointment as instructed later, but those were the only two breaks she'd taken from her keyboard and monitor.

An hour before dawn, the story was finished, edited, and ready for review by Nancy Lewis.

3

Julie enjoyed early mornings—or she had enjoyed them until the drought came. Now, even with the sun barely beginning to assert itself, the air that had always been clean and fresh and invigorating was like a wet shroud cast over the earth, and the breathing of it brought no pleasure and no promise of a new day.

Drifter stood quietly in the cross ties as Julie worked ointment into the heels of his front legs. He crunched a carrot sloppily, and the familiar grinding and the slight, sweet scent of the carrot and Drifter's healthy breath lifted Julie's spirits a bit. She performed her stall-cleaning chores automatically, almost robotically, but the physical exertion felt good after her hours in her office chair. Hefting wet, manure-laden straw with a pitchfork into a wheelbarrow wasn't exactly a membership in an exclusive health club, but the chore quickly relieved the soreness in her shoulders and back. As she wafted agricultural lime on the stall floor, she heard the tires of a car or truck rolling over the stones and dirt of her driveway.

Anyone who knows me well enough to visit at 6:00 a.m.

will know I'm in the barn, she thought, continuing with her chores. The thud of a vehicle door closing and a loud bark stopped Julie. *Danny! And look at me—hair like a tornado hit my head, lime all over my hands, teeth unbrushed* . . .

Danny used his hip to ease the big sliding door open a bit more and stepped into the barn, Sunday right behind him. "Morning," he said.

He looked like an illustration from an L.L. Bean catalog, casual, comfortable, his jeans clean, the sleeves of his chambray work shirt rolled neatly to his forearms, his face freshly shaved. In each hand he held a steaming plastic cup of coffee. "I thought I'd start my day here—take a quick look at Drifter and have coffee with his glamorous owner."

Julie chuckled. "You'll have to try the lady of the house. I'm just the barn troll."

Sunday poked his snout at Julie, his tail wagging so hard his entire back end was wiggling. She crouched and rubbed his sides. Danny waited as Julie greeted his dog, and then extended one of the cups.

"I'm real fond of barn trolls," Danny said. His smile was warm, and there was laughter in his eyes—and real fondness too, Julie thought.

"Thanks," she said as she stood up and reached for the cup of coffee. "Do you want me to bring Drifter out into the cross ties?"

Danny set his cup on the floor and selected an apple from the basket on the shelf. "Nah—I'll go in the stall. I just want to make sure everything looks OK." He stepped across the central aisle, worked the latch, and moved into the box stall with Drifter, palming the apple to the horse. Danny leaned for a moment and inspected the abraded areas to which Julie had minutes before applied the salve. "Fine," he said. "Looking good."

"Did you expect improvement this soon?" Julie asked.

Danny came out of the stall and closed the gate. "Well," he said, blushing slightly, "actually, no. I just happened to have this thermos of coffee and a couple of throwaway cups and not much to do today."

Julie laughed delightedly. "That's all the reason you need, Danny. Slow day, huh?"

"Yeah. What about you? How's the series going?"

"I guess that remains to be seen. I wrote the first piece last night, though." She paused for a moment. "If you have a few minutes, how about reading it while I shower? I'm going to run the manuscript over to Nancy at the *Express*, but I'd really like to get your opinion of it first." She was suddenly embarrassed. "If you have time, I mean. You don't have to read every word—maybe just kind of scan it, see if the premise works for you."

"Time is one thing I have a ton of today. I'd love to read it."

She set Danny up at the kitchen table with a copy of the article and the pictures and left him there with Sunday on the floor at his side. She hurried through her shower—water conservation—but dallied in her bedroom, dressing slowly. She wasn't able to keep her mind off Danny reading her article downstairs.

Two thousand and some odd words will take time to read. Why

61

is it so important to me that Danny likes what I've written? Is that because I'm unsure of my work—or unsure of Danny?

She tugged on a pair of socks, noticing that her big toe peeked pinkly back at her through a sizable hole. *Of course I'm unsure of Danny. There's nothing to be sure of at this point. But . . . he did come here to see me, not to tend to Drifter. That's good. That's very good.*

When Julie came down the stairs in fresh jeans and a summer blouse, Danny was leaning back in his chair, the pages of the article piled neatly in front of him.

"So . . . ?" Julie asked, her voice sounding tentative, almost pleading, to her own ears.

"It's . . . it's perfect, Julie. It says what lots of us think, and it's strong and articulate and . . . what? . . . *real*, I guess. The stuff about the guys out of work, and the description of the bar and those geezers killing time with the beer and whiskey . . . it's great writing."

Julie began to speak, but Danny held up his hand, stopping her.

"Let me finish, OK? The material about Dean Kendricks and how he ended up in the Bulldogger and was served even though he was underage—illegal—and what happened afterwards reads like the books of Ann Rule, the true crime writer. I could feel your emotion in the words, Julie, but the text is restrained, controlled, just as it needs to be to make the point. Great work." He picked up the top page, the one with Rick Castle gesturing from the doorway of the bar. "Great photo too. And the skid marks tell their own story. Your boss will love it. Guaranteed."

62

Julie pulled out a chair and sat down across from Danny. "Nancy handed me free rein on the series, but there are always editorial considerations. Still, I gave the piece my best shot."

"I can see that, and so will all your other readers."

She couldn't keep the smile from her face. "Thanks for taking the time to look it over, Danny. I appreciate what you've said."

He smiled back at her, and their eyes remained together for a long but not uncomfortable amount of time. "How about a celebratory dinner tonight? Burgers at the café—maybe an order of onion rings? Fried chicken? This is a special occasion—the menu is wide open to you tonight. Even a sundae for dessert, if you like."

"Wow," she said. "What a deal! But how about this? Why don't you come over at about 7:00, and I'll grill that huge steak you gave me the other day?"

"You shouldn't have to cook today, Julie. I was only joking about the café. I'd like to take you to the new restaurant over in River Falls."

Julie moved around the table to stand closer to him. "That'd be fun—but not tonight. I worked all last night on my article, and I'd really like to just have a nice meal and relax. OK?"

"I'll tell you what, then—I'll make a salad and bring the dessert." He stood and shoved his chair back under the table, standing within inches of Julie.

"Perfect," she said. "See you about 7:00, then? And I'll have a treat for Sunday too, so make sure you bring him."

Danny stepped toward Julie, closing the short distance between them, and drew her close, with his hand softly touching the back of her neck. She felt the hardness of his forearm across her shoulders and breathed in the light, masculine scent of his aftershave. They separated after a few wonderful seconds, without embarrassment, as if they'd somehow agreed to something important without actually stating it in words.

"See you then," Danny said.

Julie watched from her kitchen door as Danny, with Sunday in the passenger seat next to him, drove past the house and bumped his way down the driveway, the dust he raised hanging in the air behind his truck. She listened as he shifted smoothly through the gears—and kept on listening until there was nothing but the buzz of insects to hear. As she turned away a headline popped into her mind.

Ace Investigative Reporter Wins Nobel and Veterinarian

Julie drove down Main Street with her air conditioner on full power. It was a few minutes after 8:00, but vehicular traffic was very light and pedestrian traffic nonexistent. The time/temp clock in front of the bank read 104 F. She passed the Bulldogger and noticed perhaps a dozen cars and trucks in the parking lot. Her skid marks and those of Dean Kendricks remained etched into the surface of the street, mute testimony supporting the first article of her series. She shook her head sadly.

Poor kid—and poor, bereaved family. Why does something like this have to take place before people recognize what's happening right in front of them?

The words of Bonnie, the young waitress at the café, returned to Julie. *"Cool guy. Heck of a roper. Cute too."*

Julie flicked on her signal and turned into the *News-Express* parking lot, finding a place a few spots away from the cluster of cars and trucks already there. She was reminded of the price of her new Dodge each month when her payments were due, and she wasn't going to allow dings and dents to diminish its value.

The walk to the employee entrance was a journey through a steam bath, but the cold air inside refreshed her. She went to her cubicle and sat in front of her keyboard. A stack of mail was overflowing her in-basket, and she separated the mail quickly, tossing the junk into the wastebasket at her side. Reader mail she set aside on her desk. She answered each piece she received from those who wrote to her, regardless if they agreed or disagreed with whatever stance she'd taken in her column.

She turned on her computer and waited for it to boot up. An icon indicated that she had email, which she looked over quickly: a few cartoons sent by other staff members, a notice about a company picnic, miscellaneous spam addressed to "Dear Reporter." There was nothing worth reading or saving, and she took a perverse bit of pleasure in tapping the delete key until her screen was clear. She tucked the mail she'd set aside into her purse and stood, grabbed her leather folder, and started to her boss's office.

Nancy Lewis's door was closed, which was a very rare phenomenon. Elisha, Nancy's secretary, was drinking coffee and eating a toasted bagel.

"Morning, Leesh. Nancy busy?" Julie asked.

"Some kind of a budget meeting. A bunch of suits got here early, and they've been in with her ever since. It's supposed to go most of the day, according to Nancy." Elisha looked over at the closed door. "Nancy hates meetings. She said she'd rather have a root canal than spend a day with those bozos."

"I can't blame her." Julie smiled. "I'm glad we peons don't have to be involved in stuff like that." She took her article from her leather folder. "May I leave this with you to give to Nancy as soon as you can? It's important."

"'Course. I'll hand it to her the minute she comes out." She took the pages from Julie and glanced at the top photo, giggled for a moment, and then laughed. "That's the guy from the Bulldogger, isn't it?"

"Yep. Flattering shot, don't you think?"

"It's perfect." She paused for a moment. "Ummm . . . Can I read this?"

"Sure—help yourself. But not a word to anyone until after Nancy approves it, OK? It's the first part of my series."

"You have my word on that, Julie. Why the secrecy, though?"

"It's the first story of my series, Leesh. It's pretty hard-hitting, and I'm a little nervous about it."

Elisha waved away Julie's concern. "You're Nancy's star, Julie. She'd publish your grocery list if you submitted it."

"I doubt it." Julie laughed. "I can't afford groceries, anyway. I've got a horse to feed."

"Speaking of which, Michael has talked about nothing but Drifter since we were out to your place. He's told the other kids that Drifter is going to be his horse—that he's going to buy him from you and keep him in our garage. I was wondering if I could bring—"

"Elisha, I've told you and told you, anytime you want to bring Mike out again is fine with me. Evenings, weekends, whatever. So quit asking and just do it, will you?"

Elisha's teeth were a beautiful white against her dark skin. "You're a peach, Julie—and I'll take you up on that. Mike has a new cowboy hat he's dying to show off to you."

"Great. How about if you call first and then meet me at Maggie's ranch? I'll ride Drifter over, and Maggie has a sweet ol' mare we can put Mike on, and I'll take him out on some trails."

"He'll think he's in heaven!"

"Good. Let's do it, then."

Elisha's smile stayed with Julie, buoying her spirits until she began the walk across the parking lot to her truck. Sheets of scorching heat shimmered ahead of her like desert mirages, and the tar moved slightly under her boots. She used her key to open the door, avoiding touching the scorching chrome. She walked around the front of the truck and opened the passenger door in the same manner. There was no more breeze than there would be in an oven roasting a turkey, but at least the captured heat could escape. Leaving her windows down when she parked wasn't a good alternative; she'd spent several hundred dollars for the CD and speakers option, and she frequently left her camera in the glove compartment. Coldwater was a small town inhabited by good people, but still . . .

The thought of Danny coming at 7:00 placed a broad smile on her face as she drove home. She had the whole day ahead of her. Ordinarily, she would have been hustling home to saddle Drifter to pleasure ride and to work him a bit. Horses didn't enjoy blistering temperatures any more than humans did, but Drifter definitely needed some work, needed to run off some of his nervous energy. And another story idea had been poking at her mind, not quite announcing itself but instead giving her quick mental glimpses of it.

OK, she decided as she parked next to her barn, *Drifter needs the exercise, and so do I. Neither one of us will melt. Danny said using him wouldn't have any effect on his scratches, so why not?* She hung her camera around her neck by its leather strap before going into the barn.

Drifter seemed to think a ride was a grand idea. He left the skimpy shade of the pines in the pasture and loped over to where Julie stood at the back door of the barn shaking sweet feed in a bucket, playing the horse's favorite tune. He stood in the cross ties patiently, chomping a carrot, as she brushed him and then applied the blanket and double-rigged the western saddle. She eased the bit into his mouth after he'd swallowed his treat, placed her beat-up old Stetson on her head, filled a canteen, and led Drifter out into the sun.

Julie stood still for a moment, the slightest bit dizzy, before she stepped into a stirrup. *This is crazy—maybe we will melt.* She ground tied Drifter and went back into the barn to fill her hat with water and then run water over the outside as well. The Stetson was a tad squishy as she jammed it back on her head, but the wetness made a difference. Outside she grabbed up her reins and swung into her saddle, setting Drifter off at a quick walk.

She mused on the fortunes of the family whose land she was riding to see. Cyrus Huller and his three sons owned the largest corn operation in the county. The spring before the previous one, the Hullers had put in almost three thousand acres of feed corn. They'd done very well the year before, and they saw no reason why they wouldn't this year.

They hadn't counted on the drought lasting or doing any real damage. Julie knew that farming always involved a roll of the dice. This year, the Huller men had bet wrong, sinking most of their finances into the bumper crop they anticipated. Julie had heard rumors about their misfortune. Now, she was going to check them out. Huller land began about eight or nine miles cross-country from Julie's little ranch. That was where she was headed.

Once she'd topped a long and gradual rise, Julie had the sensation that she'd ridden out of Montana and into a foreign country. The shrill screeching of insects sawed away with an intensity that was almost violent, and certainly louder than she'd ever heard before. The woods that began a couple of miles ahead of her—once verdant and inviting—were a dusty and limp olive brown. Julie could tell from the constant flicking of Drifter's ears and the tightness of his stride that the strangeness was unsettling to him too. She turned in her saddle to look behind her, and the dust that Drifter's hooves had put into the air pointed at horse and rider like an accusing finger.

Drifter was dancing a bit, nodding his head, obviously wanting to run. Julie tapped her heels lightly against his side, and the gelding launched himself like a missile from a bazooka, scattering dirt and stones and clumps of dead grass behind him as he scrambled for traction on the baked earth. Julie leaned forward in the saddle. The healthy scent of her horse's sweat was intoxicating, and the raw speed and power of the magnificent creature under her thrilled her to her core, as it always did.

For a too-brief moment Julie was lost in the rush of the steamy air and the rhythmic, hollow-sounding *thud* of hooves against the dry earth. The speed washed away thoughts of the frustrating Danny Pulver, her sadness over the death of Dean Kendricks, and her recently completed article from her consciousness.

Julie reined Drifter down to a lope and then checked him further to an easy canter. For once, he didn't argue with her. As exhilarating as the burst of speed had been, it had sapped horse and rider.

Picking through the woods afforded shade, and maybe even a couple of degrees of temperature difference. Julie relaxed in the saddle, letting Drifter weave his way around fallen trees, rocks, and patches of mean-looking brambles.

Julie wiped her forehead with the back of her hand as

thoughts of Danny came to her mind once again. *"How about a celebratory dinner tonight?" What a sweet thought. But is he just being a good friend? Or is it more than that? He's been giving me mixed signals for well over a year. Am I looking for something in Danny that doesn't exist? Does he want a pal—a platonic sort of relationship rather than one that's based on love and closeness and sharing of lives? If that's the case, I gotta forget about him, because that's not at all what I want.*

For a moment Julie resented the marital happiness of Maggie. That her marriage was almost perfect couldn't be more obvious. Anyone near Maggie and Ian could feel the love between them, how they cherished one another.

Julie swallowed the thought and the jealousy, momentarily angry at herself for even entertaining her bitterness over the joy of two people she genuinely loved.

The forest ended abruptly. In one stride Julie and Drifter were among trees, and the next they were in the brassy sunshine. In all three directions, precise rows of three- to six-inch dull brown, desiccated spikes of corn reached for the horizon. The soil around the endless lines was almost chalky, as dry as powder, with no more life or promise to it than the scorched plants. An image of Arlington National Cemetery in Washington, D.C., appeared in Julie's mind, with the parallel columns of gleaming white crosses reaching out seemingly to the ends of the earth.

She dismounted and brought her camera to her eyes and clicked off a dozen photos, from close-ups of individual spikes to the endless rows of them. Drifter shook his head and snorted wetly. Julie took a long drink of the now warm water from her canteen and poured the rest into her hat, which she held out to her horse. Drifter sucked it dry in a couple of seconds and snorted again, demanding more.

The trek back to Julie's home wasn't a pleasure ride. She realized that she'd gone too far in the hundred-plus-degree temperature, and she was concerned about the thick lather on Drifter's chest and shoulders. He was sweating too hard for the minimal amount of work he was doing. He wasn't weaving at all—a sign of dehydration in a horse—and his ears were alert, flicking to whatever caught his interest. Nevertheless, Julie reined in and took a pinch of skin on Drifter's neck and then released it. The hide flowed back quickly, and Julie breathed a sigh of relief. If the pinched flesh had been slow to return to its normal state, she'd have known that the horse was overly fatigued and that he needed water badly.

The sight of the barn, even broiling in the sun as it was, was like a view of the Garden of Eden. Drifter tugged at the reins and danced a bit, wanting to run the last half mile to his water bucket and feed trough, but Julie held him at a sedate walk until they arrived at the barn.

After stripping off his saddle and blanket, Julie washed her horse from a large bucket of cool water, slopping it over him with a huge old sponge. Drifter grunted like a fat sow in mud as she sluiced the sweat, froth, and grime from him and then rough-dried him with an empty burlap feed sack. She turned him into his stall with a half bucket of water and a couple of generous scoops of molasses feed, and headed to her house.

She checked her watch as she left it and her camera on the dresser in her bedroom and padded off to the shower: 2:14. *Plenty of time. I can even straighten things up around here. I don't want Danny to think I'm a slob.* She grinned. *He's a neat freak. I know he is. The inside of his truck, with all his equipment and medication and supplies, is as ordered and precise as a chessboard.*

Julie's smile stayed with her through her shower and shampoo, and by the time she started getting dressed, she was humming an old Beatles tune—"Norwegian Wood." She checked the answering machine in her office and was pleased to see that the little red light wasn't flashing. *No news is good news,* she thought.

The grating howl of her old vacuum cleaner didn't irritate her as it usually did as she shoved it over her living room carpet and along the baseboards. She sucked a dust bunny the size of a snapping turtle from under her couch and found a family of them under an end table. She bundled up newspapers, horse equipment, and western wear catalogs and junk mail circulars that had accumulated on her coffee table and stuffed them into the kitchen closet.

The fresh, citrus scent of spray furniture polish lightened the muggy air, at least momentarily. Julie checked her refrigerator to make sure that her iced tea pitcher was full, and that the knucklebone she'd gotten for Sunday at the butcher shop in town was waiting for him. She looked into the freezer to determine whether or not the quart of Ben and Jerry's Cherry Garcia had escaped and found it to be in place.

She laughed at herself. *I'm like a seventeen-year-old waiting to be picked up for prom. We're going to barbecue a steak, and I feel like Danny's taking me to Paris for dinner on the Concorde.* A headline goaded her:

Giddy Reporter Wrecks Date!

Again she laughed at herself. *I'm not going to wreck anything! This is a simple get-together. Of course, it's quite possible that it could be an essential first step that could lead to something very good for both of us. Not that I'm fantasizing . . .*

⌒⌒

Danny pulled in at exactly 7:00 and parked next to Julie's truck. She watched through the kitchen window as he climbed out of his truck and motioned to Sunday, who bounded out to the ground and then watched Danny unload a huge wooden salad bowl and a bunch of wildflowers wrapped in wet newspaper. He clutched a brown paper bag in the same hand as the flowers. Julie went to the door and opened it.

"Hey, guys!"

Sunday hustled forward, dancing in front of Julie, his plumed tail thumping her legs as he moved around her. Julie crouched to welcome the dog, kneading the heavy fur just below his ears, causing him to grunt with pleasure and to draw his warm, wet tongue across her forehead.

"Looks like you've got a friend for life," Danny said. "He's usually much more reserved."

74

Julie smiled up at Danny. "He knows how I feel about him." She stood. "Come on—let's go inside."

In the kitchen, Danny held out the wildflowers to Julie. "I was at Annie Steele's place setting a broken leg on one of her goats. She said—and this is a quote—'Ain't no government flunkie gonna tell me what I can an' can't water. I've had my flower patch for better'n eighty summers, drought or no drought.' Then she insisted I take these."

Julie laughed. "She's a pistol, that Annie Steele. She's got more spirit at eighty-four than a barn full of Quarter Horse stallions."

Danny set the salad bowl on the counter. "Here's the dessert," he said as he began taking something out of the brown paper bag. "I hope you like Ben and Jerry's . . ."

"Cherry Garcia?" she asked, taking her own quart from her freezer. "I absolutely love it!" She put both quarts in the freezer. "I have a wonderful b-o-n-e for your partner. Can he have it now?"

Danny laughed. "Actually, he does know that word. He'd have been bouncing off the ceiling if you'd said it instead of spelled it. Sure—but send him outside or he'll slobber all over your floor."

Julie took the hefty bone from the refrigerator. Its meaty scent immediately reached the collie, and he stood next to Julie, staring up at her, whining very quietly. When she'd shucked the butcher paper from the treat, Sunday's whine escalated in volume and intensity. She led him to the door and out and then handed the bone to him, impressed with how gently he received it from her hand even though he was drooling copiously.

"Thanks, Julie. It was nice of you to think of Sunday," Danny said.

"He's my buddy." Julie smiled. "Want to have an iced tea before we start the fire?"

They sat in the living room, Danny on a love seat across from Julie on the couch. Her oscillating fan did little more than stir the thick, overheated air, but the conversation flowed naturally.

"Great iced tea," Danny commented. "Strong enough to melt a horseshoe, which is fine with me. That's my pet peeve—weak iced tea and weak hot coffee."

Julie smiled. "That's your only pet peeve?"

"I don't have many of them, actually," Danny answered seriously. "Life is too short to let little things mess up a day—or even a minute." He shifted uncomfortably in the love seat.

"Do you want to sit over here and I'll take the love seat? Is it too soft for you?"

Color suffused Danny's face. "It's not the furniture. I was, well ... um ... butted today while I was bending over Annie Steele's goat."

"Butted?"

"Butted in the butt, I'm sad to say. That nanny goat hit me like an express train. I thought Annie was going to fall over from laughing so hard. And, knowing her, everybody in town will know about it by now."

Julie bit back a giggle. "Are you OK?" she asked. "Were you hurt?"

"Just my pride, I guess. But I'll tell you what: I won't be going riding for a few days."

"Could have been worse, I suppose. I saw a goat at the Summer Barrel Racing Finals a couple of years ago whack a Chevy Blazer, and he punched in an entire door panel, even broke the window from the impact."

"Yeah," Danny said. "For a relatively small animal, a goat can generate an amazing amount of power in a headlong charge." He sipped some iced tea. "You know," he said contemplatively, "this is something I never get tired of."

"What do you mean?"

"Listen for a minute."

She did so, cocking her head slightly, closing her eyes, still not sure what Danny meant. "I don't hear a thing," she said after a moment.

"That's exactly my point. The quiet—the peace—that's such an inherent part of this area. It's something really special. I've come home after a dozen or so hours of treating animals that didn't at all want to be treated, of driving too many miles, drinking too much coffee, and missing a meal or two. And then I sit out in back of my place and watch the sunset, and all the stress and tension and aggravation just kind of drift off, like a storm cloud being chased by a breeze."

"I know exactly what you mean," Julie said. "I've had the same sort of thing happen. I wouldn't care to live anywhere else in the world."

"Neither would I. When I finished veterinary school I knew I could join a big city practice and make a ton of money and have all the toys and so forth—maybe open an equine-only clinic and treat the hunter-jumpers for the jet set. But that would've been a totally different sort of life, and not one I wanted to pursue." He sighed contentedly. "I'll take a fence to put my feet on and a lawn chair and my dog next to me over a swimming pool and martinis in suburbia any day."

Julie nodded. "Me too. I'll take my small-town newspaper and my home and life here over anything the big city presses could offer me. I'll never get rich, but I don't really care about that. I'll never get a bleeding ulcer or have to gobble pills to be able to stand myself, either."

"I guess we both know what we want—what's important to us," Danny said. "There are lots of people who don't."

The silence that followed was an intimate one, and a comfortable one that lasted a few delicious seconds. Then Julie cleared her throat and asked, "Ready for dinner?"

"You bet—but there's one thing you haven't mentioned yet."

"Oh? What's that?"

"Your article. How did your boss like your story?"

Julie stood. "I really don't know. I dropped it off to Nancy this morning, and I haven't heard anything from her, so . . . well . . . I'm not sure, I guess."

"I'm sure, though—she had to love it," Danny said. "And if there was a problem with it, you'd have heard by now, right?"

"I guess so."

"Of course you would. Come on—let's cook that steak!"

A short while later, they sat down to dinner. Danny's salad was a work of art: crisp romaine lettuce, fresh Spanish onion, thick tomato slices, tiny radishes, baby carrots, bits of provolone cheese, all bathed in a rich, sweet but sharp Italian dressing. The steak was superb, with just enough marbling of fat to make it sizzle enticingly on the charcoal grill. Crusty chunks of Italian bread, tugged and torn rather than sliced from the loaf Julie had picked up at the grocery, complemented the beef and the salad perfectly. Sunday, just outside the kitchen door with his knucklebone between his forepaws, gnawed away happily as the humans ate at the kitchen table.

When their plates were empty, Julie pushed back from the table and asked, "Coffee—strong coffee? Or do you want ice cream now?"

Danny held up his hands in surrender. "I'm never going to eat anything ever again—but coffee sounds perfect."

"Why don't you go into the living room while I brew up a pot? It won't take a minute."

"Can I help you clean up a bit?"

"There's not much to do. Go on—I'll be right out with our coffee."

"Fair enough," Danny said. "Look—I know it's still hotter than blazes out, but would you like to go for a walk in a while?"

"Yes—yes I would. I was just kind of thinking the same thing. The moon should be almost full. It'll be pretty."

≈≈≈

The moon, just as Julie had said, was close to full. But it seemed to have a rare luminescence to it this night, as if it had grown in size and moved much closer to the earth. The shadows and craters seemed more precisely defined, and the light was pure and opalescent and subdued and fell on them softly, like a loving mother's touch.

Danny's hand found Julie's as they started up a slight grade following the pasture fence. Their palms met naturally, and their fingers interlocked gently as they walked. Sunday trip-tropped along beside the couple, stopping every so often to raise his nose to check the scents of the night.

"Seems like the temperature's gone down a few degrees," Danny observed. "I've been sitting outside late at night a lot, and it's rare that I've felt a temperature change."

"Can't sleep in the heat?" Julie asked.

"Not real well, no. I can't afford to have my place rewired to carry an air conditioner, and even if I could, I can't afford the unit." He laughed. "So I sit outside and watch Sunday chase fireflies until he gets tired of that. Then he comes and sits next to me."

"A little lonely?" Julie asked, and then wished she'd kept her mouth shut.

"Sunday? No." He laughed. "I take him with me every day—no reason for him to be lonely."

Julie pushed Danny's shoulder playfully with her free hand. "You, I mean—ya goof."

"Sometimes," Danny admitted, and then qualified his answer with an "I guess. I don't think much about it." He waited a moment and then asked, "You?"

They took a few more steps before Julie answered. "At times. My life is full, and I have wonderful friends, and the church, and Drifter and barrel racing, and all that. I love my work. I'm content, really—and grateful for the life I have. But some nights I come home and there's nothing there, you know? I mean all my stuff is there, but that's what it is—stuff."

"What do you do on those nights?" Danny asked.

"I usually go out to the barn. This is probably dumb, but I pull up a bale of straw and sit in the dark and listen to Drifter breathe and move around in his stall and snort at me." She built up a thought in her mind for a full minute before speaking again. "It's the idea of having a living creature near me who loves me and depends on me and genuinely wants to have me around, I think. It makes me feel better."

"It's not dumb at all, Julie," Danny said so quietly that she barely heard the words. They stopped at the top of the rise, where the pasture fence veered off to the left on its way down the grade. A shooting star flashed across the sky, its shimmering tail streaking south to north.

"Beautiful," Julie breathed. The stars seemed close enough to touch, their glitter profoundly bright, as intense as the facets of a perfectly cut diamond. She leaned against her fence and released Danny's hand. "There's such beauty in the world, and sometimes it's easy to forget that."

He moved a step closer. "It's a shame we don't see that beauty more often. It's always there, but we're too busy with minutia to pay attention to it."

And then he was kissing her. Julie felt suspended in space, no longer part of the world, and her entire universe became the sensation of Danny Pulver's lips on hers, his closeness, the strength of his body, the texture of the shaggy hair at the back of his collar where her hand rested.

They parted wordlessly and by unspoken consent began back down the hill. Danny put his arm around her waist, and she held him in the same manner. Sunday bounded past them, anxious to get back to his bone.

When they stood at the kitchen door, Julie grinned at Danny. "Cherry Garcia time?"

"Absolutely." Danny smiled back at her.

As Julie flicked on the kitchen light, the telephone rang. She held up a finger to Danny and took the receiver from the wall. "Julie Downs."

"Julie—Nancy Lewis. I hate to bother you at home this late, but it's important. I need you to come in to the office now—as soon as you can get here." Nancy's tone of voice made it clear that she wasn't issuing a request, that Julie had next to no choice in the matter.

"I'll be there in fifteen minutes, Nancy," she said.

Nancy broke the connection.

Julie turned to Danny. "That was my boss," she said. "I've got to go to the office."

4

Ten-thirty on a Friday night and Nancy calls me into the office. It wasn't a request either. It was an order. So. My piece didn't knock her socks off. That's no big deal. I can fix it, bring it up to whatever standards Nancy wants.

Julie swallowed hard. *But couldn't it have waited until Monday? What's she doing at her office at this time of night?*

Confusing and contradictory thoughts chased one another frantically through Julie's mind as she drove to Coldwater. Nancy's voice had sounded neither angry nor pleased. Rather, she was businesslike, just as she always was. She sounded tired, maybe, but that was the only difference Julie could discern.

Julie's high beams picked up a pair of eyes—and then another set—at the roadside twenty or so yards ahead. They glowed strangely, and then there was a flash of white below one set of eyes—light reflecting off the teeth of a large coyote. Julie's headlights pinned the animals for a second: a big one, about the size of Sunday, and another standing next to him, a few inches shorter at the shoulder. The larger coyote stood near some roadkill in the center of the street.

The smaller coyote spun away into the brush as Julie's truck came closer. The larger one made another attempt to drag the roadkill free, but it was stuck to the soft tar of the road. Julie hit her horn. The coyote flashed his teeth at her again and then was gone. She noticed how thin the haunches of the predator were, how clearly defined his ribs. *Even the coyotes are hurting from the drought,* she thought.

Julie rolled past the Bulldogger. The thumping bass line from a blaring heavy metal number on the jukebox created a physical sensation, even in the cab of her truck with the windows closed. Ken Townsend in his sleek cruiser passed her and flashed his lights. She raised her hand in a wave.

Several cars and trucks still sat in the *News-Express* lot, but Julie was able to park her truck within a few steps of the rear door of the building. She noticed Nancy's red Toyota Celica in the spot marked "Mng. Editor"; next to it, she saw a barge-sized blue Lincoln Town Car she didn't recognize. She looked up at the building before walking to the door. A newspaper of any size never sleeps—but most of the windows were dark.

Julie straightened her shoulders and used her after-hours key card to open the door. She stopped to take a long drink from a fountain and then headed down the corridor to Nancy's office. She saw that the door was open this time. Murmurs of voices reached Julie from her boss's office, and some of the words were strident, but she couldn't make out the context.

Julie tapped on the door frame.

"Here she is," Nancy said to the man sitting on the couch to the side of her desk. "Come on in, Julie."

Nancy looked rumpled and tired—and angry. Her usually orderly desktop was littered with papers and empty Styrofoam coffee cups. Prominent among the papers—directly in front of Nancy—was Julie's article. The man stood up from the couch.

"Julie," Nancy said, "this is Chad Worther. He's from the corporate counsel office of the fine folks who own the *News-Express*."

Worther looked distinguished and quite fresh and crisp. His suit fit him perfectly, moved with him as he extended his hand to Julie, hugged the back of his neck and shoulders with no off-the-rack gap. His hair, a flowing mane of pure white, looked both casual and at the same time freshly barbered. His eyes were an icy blue that conveyed none of the warmth that his smile indicated. Julie estimated his age at about sixty.

"Ms. Downs," Worther said, "I'm so pleased to meet you. I'm very impressed with your writing."

Nancy snorted. "Cut the hype, Chad. Tell Julie that you're here to step on our First Amendment rights and that we can't run her story."

Julie took the attorney's hand. His grasp was firm and dry. "Please have a seat, Ms. Downs," he said, releasing her hand. Julie took the chair facing Nancy's desk and waited for an explanation.

Nancy broke the silence. "Chad was here with the budget guys today," she said, her voice weary and a bit scratchy. "I showed him your story. By the way, I think it's quite good, particularly in the context of effective writing—of arguing your points coherently and articulately. If it were up to me, Julie, you and I would be tweaking some of the points and tightening the structure and blocking it out to run next Wednesday." She paused and took a breath. "But it isn't up to me." She made eye contact with Julie. "I'm genuinely sorry."

It took a heartbeat for Julie to assimilate what she'd just heard. She had to force her words, to struggle to keep her voice even. "What's the problem? What do I need to fix or change?"

"The problem, Ms. Downs," Worther said, "isn't in your writing, necessarily. It's far more a matter of legal liability. You accuse a business owner of serving a minor illegally, and you have absolutely no proof of your allegations. You portray a place of business as a foul cave frequented by drooling drunks and frustrated and hostile farm workers. The picture of the owner is scandalous, and the pictures of the road prove nothing beyond the fact that there are skid marks on it. The article is like a tabloid—and not something that the people to whom I report will allow to be printed."

"It's a matter of degree," Nancy Lewis added, looking at Julie. "Your readers have come to expect your own perspectives on the matters you cover—and that's a big part of why your column has become so popular. You were involved in this story—part of it happened right in front of you. I think, many times, a writer has to go with his or her heart, which you've obviously done here, Julie. Otherwise, stories and features become mechanical and without the life and spirit readers demand."

The attorney leaned back on the couch and placed an artificial smile on his face. "Ms. Lewis has advised our offices of your excellent work on your column and on the many features you've written. We need people like you, but you must realize that this is the age of the lawsuit and court-room giveaways that total millions in cases such as these." He increased the size of his smile. "Now, what I'd like to have happen, Ms. Downs, is for you to put this Bull-Runner situation and that poor boy out of your mind and focus on the sort of writing that—"

Nancy stood up behind her desk. "Chad," she said, "I don't need you counseling or advising my staff—that's my job. And I certainly don't need you giving them orders. I've listened to you all evening, and now I need you to listen to me. Please leave."

Worther stood and turned to her. "Perhaps you've forgot-ten who signs your rather generous paycheck, Nancy."

"There won't be any paycheck to sign unless you leave immediately. One more word and you'll find my letter of resignation on my desk Monday morning. Don't attempt to intimidate me, Chad, because you'd have a terrible time explaining how you pushed the best managing editor the *News-Express* has ever had out of her job. Now go, so I can talk with my reporter."

Worther picked up his briefcase, checked the lock on it, and then left the office without speaking or even looking at Nancy or Julie. The two women listened to his footsteps recede down the corridor.

"Well," Julie said. "I guess that's that."

Nancy sighed. "Yes, it is. The problem is, that fatuous clown is right. There's a multitude of legal issues involved in your article. That's not to say that I didn't love it—because I did. But Chad was correct. This is the age of the lawsuit. I doubt that Rick Castle is the money behind the Bulldogger and the other joints like it. They'd bring a suit the second the *Express* hit the street, and they'd win."

"If that's the case, why did you haul me in here?"

Nancy sighed again. "Let's call it a learning experience for you. I wanted you to see an aspect of journalism you may not have been aware of. People like Worther abound in communications and, sadly, they're powerful. If it came down to a face-off between me and Worther, he'd win. The owners would dump me in a minute. And since I made my feelings about you and your work clear to Chad, I suspect you'd get the boot at the same time I did."

"But . . . but you threatened the guy, Nancy."

"Sure I did. I meant to. The thing is, he's not quite sure enough of himself to take this to the big money people." She picked up Julie's manuscript, gazed at it for a moment, and dropped it back onto her desk. "There's another and more important reason I dragged you here tonight, Julie. I didn't want to wait for the weekend to pass without letting you know what I think of your article. I'm expecting more big things from you. I mean that. But on this one . . . well . . . we lose."

Julie sat quietly for a moment. "Some alterations, Nancy. Maybe if I just—"

Nancy shook her head. "Sorry."

Julie stood. Her voice was the slightest bit shaky when she spoke. "OK. I've got another idea I'm working on." She faced her boss for a long moment. "OK," she repeated. "Good night, Nancy."

Julie sat behind the wheel of her truck, staring at the *News-Express* building. After a long moment she cranked her engine, backed out of the parking space, and drove across the mostly empty lot, the white demarcations appearing pure and bright against the blackness of the asphalt.

It happens. Every reporter gets a story squelched once in a while. It's not that big of a deal, and the Huller failed crop story will work. I learned something, just like Nancy hoped I would. I can't allow myself to feel that I'm a knight in shining armor. I'm a reporter—a journalist. I deal in facts, not feelings or emotions. I made myself out to be cop, judge, and jury on the story—and that's where I blew it.

She turned toward town from the newspaper lot, not quite ready to go home.

She knew she had been too involved in the story. She should have called the police as soon as the Kendricks kid almost hit her. That was the bottom line—and that was why she wrote that story. But guilt didn't make for good journalism.

She recalled a seminar she'd attended a few years ago on

objectivity in writing. "Don't hate the bad guys and don't fall in love with the good guys," the speaker had said. "Capture them, hold them up naked to your readers, tell the story—and end it right there."

Drago's lights were still on—the café was open late to catch the after-movie daters and those who sought refuge from the heat or from loneliness. Ken's Ford glinted under the streetlight to the left of the front door. Julie parked next to it.

Why am I doing this? Julie asked herself. The fact that she had no real answer didn't stop her.

A pair of young couples sat in a front booth, drinking milkshakes and laughing about the movie they'd just seen. A couple of cowhands drank coffee at the counter while talking quietly to one another. Ken sat alone in a booth to the rear, staring into a cup of coffee, a slice of pie sitting untouched on a plate next to his silent police radio.

Julie stopped next to the police officer. "Hey, Ken," she said.

He glanced up quickly, almost as if she'd awakened him, and smiled. "Julie—good to see you. Have a seat."

She slid into the booth across from him. "You were deep in thought," she said. "That's exactly what I'm trying to avoid—thinking."

"Sounds bad," Ken said. "Anything I can help with?"

"I guess it's not so bad—just work stuff."

"Me too. Maybe we should start a club."

She looked up at Ken. His eyes were warm and deep and

blue—and somehow Julie felt a bit better. "What's up? Or, shouldn't I ask?" She laughed a bit self-consciously.

"Not at all. I'm glad you're here. After all, we've shared our deepest secrets." He forced a smile. "Do you know Ross Craig—the police chief?" Julie nodded. "Seems like there's a bit of personality conflict between us," Ken continued. "And guess who always loses in that kind of clash—the new patrol cop or the head honcho?"

"Whew," Julie breathed. "I see your point. Maybe it's because you're so new to the PD. It takes time for people to work comfortably together."

"It's a bit more basic than that, I think," Ken said. He looked back into his coffee cup. "I shouldn't be talking about this stuff. I like Coldwater a lot, and I like the job a lot. Things will work out."

"I'm sure they will. But I need to tell you this: anything you say to me is off the record."

He nodded. "Let me get you coffee or something. Ice cream?"

"Iced tea with lemon would be great." Julie watched Ken walk to the counter and noticed how the eyes of everyone in the café followed him. *He must be conscious of it,* she thought, *but he's as comfortable as he'd be if he were all alone here.*

Ken set the tall glass in front of Julie. "So," he said, sitting down again on his side of the booth, "your turn to tell me your woes."

It didn't take Julie more than a few minutes to tell her story.

91

"Sounds like your boss supported you," he said. "She sounds like a gutsy lady."

"She's great. I can't say enough in favor of her."

Ken glanced at his watch. "I'm sorry about the story," he said. "I know the Bulldogger is a cesspool, but there's not a whole lot I can do about it right now." He grinned at her for a moment and added, "Don't toss any of your notes, OK?" He pushed out from behind the table. "Gotta run. I'm glad you stopped, Julie."

His right hand began to move toward her hand, resting on the table, and then it returned to its place at his side.

"Me too, Ken. 'Night." Again Julie watched Ken Townsend walk away—and again all the eyes in the café followed him.

Julie clicked on her turn signal at the mouth of her driveway from habit, although there probably wasn't another vehicle on her road within a dozen miles. She parked in her usual place next to the barn and turned off her engine. She glanced at the clock on the dash: 12:04 a.m. She opened her door but remained behind the wheel, staring off restlessly into the night. When she did leave the truck, the thud of her closing the door sounded amplified, much louder than usual in the steamy silence. Instead of going to her house, Julie began walking her fence line, taking the same path she'd followed, hand-in-hand with Danny, a few hours before.

A sort of mist hung now in the air, but it was different from the dew that rose from the ground before the drought began. Morning was still far off, but the unrelenting heat drew the minute bits of moisture that existed in the parched soil and carried it away selfishly, cruelly.

The fence curved and wandered off to the east. Julie stopped. After a minute she sat down on the crusty grass and leaned against the corner pole. The rough cedar felt good and strong against her back, and she extended her legs out in front of her and settled into the dirt. The night—even with its smothering blanket of heat—felt good.

Julie thought about how she'd left things with Danny earlier that night, after the telephone call from Nancy. *I must have looked stricken—because I was.*

"That was Nancy Lewis. I've got to go to the office."

"I'll drive you—I can wait in my truck while you take care of your business."

"No—thanks, but no. This isn't going to be good news."

"You don't know that. Look—I'll wait here, OK?"

"It's late, Danny. I need to . . . I don't know. I need some time to assimilate whatever's going on."

"Maybe I could—"

"I've got to go, Danny."

Danny had nodded, his eyes still on hers. The deep chestnut gaze looked flat. He had turned and left, the screen door flapping into place behind him.

Julie picked a bug of some kind off the back of her neck and flicked it away. The fireflies were pretty much done for the night, but a few lingerers still flashed and glowed above the parched grass.

Why didn't I let him wait for me? Why did I chase him off

93

like that—like a casual friend who was getting in the way of something important? What makes me do that? Am I trying to prove how tough and independent I am? I'm not tough at all, and that's what I need to keep people from seeing. But not Danny Pulver. I want him to see who I am.

He kissed me here, right by this fence post. Holding him was wonderful.

But I wouldn't let him wait for me.

She pushed herself to her feet, wiping her arm across her eyes.

Unbidden and acutely unwanted, a headline sprang up in Julie's mind:

Failed Writer Refuses Closeness with Dr. D. Pulver
Spends Life Alone Writing Ad Copy for Al's Grocery

And Officer Friendly? What's that all about? I'm about as impetuous as an adding machine—yet I pulled in next to his car at Drago's as if I was drawn by a magnet. I just met the man!

As she headed down the slope, Julie stubbed her toe on a protruding stone. "Stupid rock!" she yelled, and launched it back up the hill with a swift and well-directed kick. A jolt of pain shot from her big toe up her leg, and she yelped in pain.

Another sound froze her in place—the insistent, blood-chilling *burr* of small pebbles being shaken in a tin can. Her toe pain forgotten, Julie broke from her statue-like stillness to a full-out gallop down the hill and didn't slow until she stood panting in front of her kitchen door.

She sucked in huge gulps of the sticky night air, and it

seemed to take forever to fill her lungs and slow her breathing. The rattlesnake's warning sounded again in her ears, as real as it had been a half mile away. She took another deep breath and let her shoulders—her entire posture—slump wearily.

"What a swell night," she said aloud. She started to her house, favoring the sore toe and limping slightly. "And," she grumbled, "I've been putting off my research."

Feeling slightly like a martyr but knowing she owed her working stories some thought and some computer time, she planted herself in her chair in front of her desk. She used her *News-Express* password to access the newspaper's various subscription-only search engines and typed in a keyword to begin her search, marveling, as she always did, at the efficiency of the system. Almost instantaneously, she was offered well over seventeen thousand citations on her topic, Quarter Horse breeding in Montana. She scrolled through the sites and works offered, sending those she liked to her printer. When the machine stopped its laser-whine several minutes later, Julie collected the pages and settled back in her chair to begin reading. As usual, she fell into her work, unconscious of the passing time.

The next morning Julie was amazed to find she'd slept through the heat of the night without waking. She pushed back the sheet she'd covered herself with, rubbed the sleep from her eyes, swung her feet to the floor—and then stopped. Something was wrong. Instead of the unremitting barrage of light and heat she was accustomed to each morning since the drought began, everything was covered with a subtle grayness, a weak and washed-out hue instead of the normally brassy sunshine. The heat hadn't dissipated. The air remained dense, making her bedroom seem claustrophobic, as if the walls had closed in on her overnight. She glanced at her bedside clock: 8:03.

Could I have slept the night and the day—and it's now evening? She shook her head, trying to clear it. *I've never done that, no matter how tired I've been. And Drifter would've been carrying on out in his stall and I'd have heard him. This is weird . . .*

She clicked on the radio on her dresser. Instead of the mindless babble of the morning team at CWKX she'd anticipated, the voice she heard was deep, sonorous, certainly not local talent.

". . . Weather Bureau," the voice continued. "The storm originated in the Dakotas late last night and has been moving east to west at an erratic rate of speed, apparently gathering power. Although the wind velocity is not currently a major problem, gusts up to sixty miles per hour are not uncommon as the mass moves toward upper Montana. Because of the prevailing drought conditions, the dehydrated soil is being stripped from the earth and swept in front of the storm in a monumental cloud that is obscuring the sun in many areas." The announcer paused for a moment.

"I repeat: if the storm reaches your location, stay in your home. Do not allow children or pets to go outside. Any farm animals that can be brought into barns should be tended to immediately. Do not attempt to drive a car or truck or operate a tractor during the storm, should it reach you. In older homes, stuffing towels around loose-fitting windows is advised. Close all windows and doors as firmly as possible. Electric and telephone services may well be disrupted. We strongly suggest that you fill large jugs, bottles, kettles, whatever you have, with water if your source of water is a well. Again, do not attempt to . . ."

The voice crackled and fizzled away to a steady hum, which stopped abruptly after a minute or so. Julie put on a pair of jeans and a shirt and hauled on her boots, ignoring the throbbing of her toe from its collision with the stone the night before. A sound stopped her in mid-motion: a gentle, sloughing sound like a friendly night rain. But Julie knew immediately that it wasn't rain. It was wind-driven desiccated soil.

She raced down the stairs and out the kitchen door. Her exposed skin—hands, face, and neck—began itching and then burning within a few steps of her home. It was as if she'd been drenched in an acid of some sort—not caustic enough to raise blisters but strong enough to cause extreme discomfort. Julie's eyes began to tear copiously, making her vision shimmery and indistinct. Specks of soil almost too small to see felt like fiery cinders in her eyes. She lumbered toward the barn, attempting to shield her eyes with cupped hands.

The wind was strong enough to make her steps a stumbling charade of a normal gait. She stopped, covered her eyes as completely as she could with her hands, and let her tears do their natural job of cleansing. Blinking, she realized, was a part of the process, but each open-and-shut motion felt like her eyes were being scrubbed with sandpaper.

Julie waited a full minute and then peeked out through a minute slit between a pair of fingers. She was surprised to see that she wasn't facing her barn as she thought she was. One of her stumbles had turned her on a tangent from the building, facing her toward her pasture fence. She corrected her position and charged forward to the barn, hands clasped over her eyes.

She heard Drifter when she was still several strides away. He was squealing in that high-pitched, frantic scream that panicked horses find within themselves, and the booming impact of hooves against wood hurried Julie to the big door. She leaned into it, sliding it only wide enough to squeeze herself through, and then pulled it shut from the inside. Although she'd been outside and exposed to the storm for mere minutes, the interior of the barn seemed like a totally different and wonderfully safe world—except for Drifter thrashing in his stall. Julie snapped on the overhead light and ran down the central aisle to her horse's stall, her eyes again running tears and grinding painfully as she blinked.

Drifter was dripping nervous sweat. He was rearing, striking with his forefeet at the wall off his stall, his panic and his instinct demanding that he do what horses have always done in times of fright—run away from whatever was threatening him.

The artificial light changed the texture of the illumination in the barn, making it something Drifter knew wouldn't harm him, and Julie's voice brought him down yet further. She stood outside his stall, talking to the horse, praising him, singing to him. She had been around horses for too many years to go into a stall with one who was coming apart, regardless of how much she loved the animal. Twelve hundred pounds against a hundred and thirty wasn't an even match.

After several minutes of talking and then singing to Drifter, Julie held an apple out to him. His eyes were still opened wider than normal, and his muscles were as tight as bands of iron, but he accepted the treat. She quickly gave him another, and the familiarity of chomping his favorite treat calmed him noticeably. Julie began preparing the stall across the aisle to hold Drifter as she mucked his usual stall. She couldn't trust him not to tear the cross ties out of the walls if something spooked him, and was still leery about working in his stall with the horse next to her.

The barn creaked and moaned, indicating the wind was increasing in strength. The massive front door rattled on its track, but both Julie and Drifter had heard that sound before, during the winter, when the wind had shrieked like a ghostly freight train and stinging sleet had flown horizontally past the windows. She remembered the storm that had taken place several Thanksgivings ago—the worst blizzard in 150 years, the Montana Weather Bureau had called it. She'd strung a rope from the house to the barn just before the storm howled in with its eighty-mile-per-hour winds and over five feet of snow. The thought of following that rope, hand over hand in a disorienting blur of white, in wind that would have blown her into the storm like a discarded newspaper if she lost her grip or if the rope broke, made her shudder.

Julie tossed a lead line over Drifter's neck and led the now relatively calm Quarter Horse into the stall she'd prepared. Drifter sank his head into the feed bucket as she latched the stall gate. The lights flickered. Drifter's head snapped up; bits of crimped oats and molasses-coated corn dribbled from his mouth as he looked around himself, seeking an escape. Julie began talking again in a low, calm voice, and reached out to touch the animal's shoulder. The lights wavered again for a quick moment and then, blessedly, stayed on. As Drifter calmed and returned to his feed, Julie walked to a window and leaned her elbows on its frame, staring through the glass at the storm.

It was barely 9:00 in the morning, but the world around her was as dark as the end of a cloudy, rainy day. The swirling of the dirt-laden wind was almost hypnotic. She felt herself being drawn into the maelstrom—her mind being carried along with it. In the semi-darkness of the whirling grit, patterns developed and then became indistinct images. Julie's shoulders relaxed and she shifted her boots to a more comfortable position without really being conscious of doing so.

The spinning images became a bit more distinct, became at first places—her bedroom when she was a child, her college dorm—and then faces: her dad smiling at her, her first boss after college . . . and Roger. She hadn't thought of him in a while, yet he seemed to persist in popping, totally unbidden, into her mind every so often.

A half dozen years ago she'd had a man in her life. Roger

Phillips was a guy with too much inherited money and too little to do with his time. He'd bought an operating cattle ranch from an elderly couple outside of Coldwater, and he'd set about to increase the profits of the ranch, to make it run at peak efficiency, to make it a model for modern agriculture. He'd fired the four cowhands who had been with the old couple for several years, and hired some drifters whom he could pay low wages. Roger bought stock without knowing cattle, with price per head more important to him than hardiness, fecundity, and weight yield.

Julie, for reasons she still didn't completely understand, had been fascinated with Roger Phillips. Coldwater had accepted Roger almost immediately. He'd donated large amounts of money to the church, although he wasn't a member, and financed a trip to Billings for the high school rodeo team to compete in the state finals. He rarely drank alcohol, and when he did so, his choice was a glass of dry white wine. He was well aware of Julie's faith and her moral beliefs, and he abided by them. Roger was bright—with an Ivy League degree in philosophy—and articulate and very good looking. He treated Julie as if she were a queen—and Julie reveled in it.

Julie had been in a dream world for several months. On her birthday he'd chartered a small jet and had taken her to Helena for dinner at a lavish restaurant, then to a sold-out Sting concert, where they'd had front row center seats, and then back home the same night.

The fascination—the infatuation—had ended for Julie as rapidly as it had begun. Roger Phillips, she abruptly came to realize, was as boring as stacked wood.

The entire episode seemed like it had taken place a long time ago, but it left an imprint on Julie that she knew would be with her forever. In life and in relationships, there was no such thing as a free ride. Fun and games and fancy toys don't equal real love.

Pulling herself out of the mesmerizing effects of the dust storm required a physical effort. She had to turn her face from the window to reorder her thoughts, to push Roger out of her consciousness, to orient herself to the reality of the day. She picked up a Jan Karon novel from a shelf where she'd left it a few nights ago and dragged a bale of straw down the aisle to Drifter's stall. The horse was relaxed, snuffling through the flake of hay she'd tossed to him, apparently at peace with the world.

Until the lights flicker or go out again.

Julie sat on the straw and opened the book to the page she'd dog-eared, but this time, Karon failed to grab Julie's interest. The words swam on the page, and after beginning the same paragraph four times, Julie closed the book. She stretched her legs out in front of her and snuggled her back a little more comfortably. Her injured toe throbbed a bit, but with no weight on it, it felt better. Her eyes felt rough and abraded, and it was less painful to simply keep them closed.

A thump and then the screech of the front door of the barn jerked Julie from her doze. She stood as Sunday squeezed through the opening, followed in a moment by Danny. The collie didn't dash up to greet Julie as usual. Instead, he stood staring up at Danny, his tail tucked a bit between his rear legs and his tongue hanging from the side of his mouth.

"Whew," Danny said, rubbing his eyes. "I've never seen anything like this before."

Julie hurried up the aisle to the man and the dog. "Still real bad?" she asked. "I've been out here all morning with Drifter."

"Still bad, yeah," Danny said. "Animals don't like this sort of thing." He pointed to Sunday. "Lookit this poor guy."

Julie crouched next to the collie and saw his widened eyes and the rapidity of his breathing. Saliva dripped from his tongue to the floor of the barn. She saw, too, that he stood with his knees slightly flexed, like a dog cringing from a punishment. When she stroked him she felt his body tremble. She hugged him closer, and he buried his face against her.

"How were you able to drive, Danny?" She glanced over at a window. "I couldn't even see my fence through the storm."

Danny grinned and began slapping dust from his jeans and shirt. "Fog lights and good luck. I was in first gear all the way from Bobby Allen's place to here. I had to stop a million times when I couldn't see anything at all."

"Sounds dangerous. You didn't have to come . . ."

"I wanted to, Julie." He crouched down and wrapped both the woman and the dog in a hug.

Julie sighed. "I'm glad you did."

They stood up together, Sunday still between them.

"What happened at the *Express* last night? I'd hoped you'd call when you got in."

"I'm sorry that I didn't. Come on—pull up a bale of straw, and we can talk."

Danny placed a bale next to Julie's and sat down. Sunday quivered in front of them, pressed closely against their legs, as Julie related the entire story—including her meeting with Ken Townsend. There was a quick flicker of something in Danny's eyes when she mentioned the cop, but he didn't speak.

". . . and felt like a dummy for kicking that rock, and I came back here and fell into bed, and when I woke up this morning, there was all this." She waved an arm around her.

Danny fiddled with a piece of straw before he spoke. "I'm really sorry about the story. It was good and effective writing, and the legalities can't diminish that."

Julie moved a couple of inches closer to Danny, and their shoulders touched lightly. She dropped her hand to Sunday's back and kneaded his coat. "It all seems so one-sided, so stupid," she agreed. "That boy is dead, and I can't write about what killed him. Of course it was foolish of Dean to drive drunk—but the fact that he was served illegally needs to be pointed out to people so that we can make certain the same thing doesn't happen again. That's what's so frustrating about this—not the fact that my work won't be published, but that people will know only what happened, not how and why it happened."

"Maybe another story, Julie? One that comes to the same conclusions a bit obliquely, so there's no legal hassle?"

Julie exhaled. "I don't think so. After that lawyer's involvement, and what Nancy said afterward, I think it's a dead subject for me."

"Well, I guess that's that, then," Danny said. After a moment, he asked, "What's next? The series wasn't terminated, was it?"

"No—not at all. I'm going out to talk with Cyrus Huller within the next couple of days. I rode over to the edge of his land and took a bunch of photos of his fields."

"Bad?"

"Hideous. Acre after acre of dead corn spikes. It was like a desert—and that's not an exaggeration. Anyway, Cyrus has been around here for a long time. I hope I can get some first-person history from him, and if the interview goes well, I'll lead the series with that."

Danny began to respond when a gust throttled the barn, shaking beams and rattling windows and frames. The lights wavered but recovered. Long-undisturbed dust and bits of bird's nest drifted to the floor from the interior of the roof. Drifter snorted and backed into the corner of his stall.

"Wind's getting stronger," Danny said. "Are all the windows closed in your house? Doors shut tightly?"

Julie was on her feet. "I think so. I didn't pay much attention when I came to the barn. I didn't think I'd—"

Another blast of wind struck the barn. "Your house is going to be a sandbox if there's any way for the dirt to get in," Danny said. "I'd better go check. I'll go out the front, and you close the door after me. We don't want the wind to catch it and rip it off the—"

"No, Danny! You're not going out there!" Even to Julie's own ears her voice sounded on the cusp of panic.

"Hey—OK, Julie," Danny said, holding up his hands in mock surrender. "I won't go out. But I'll tell you this: there's going to be a monumental amount of cleaning to do when the storm's over. And, from the looks of things, it's going to be a long, long day stuck here in the barn."

Julie exhaled audibly, and her smile was a bit tremulous. "I didn't mean to shriek like that, but the wind and the storm have me right on edge. How long do these things last? Maybe it'll die down soon, and we—"

Something metal, possibly a trash can from the sound of it, slammed into the side of the barn with an impact like that of a battering ram striking a sheet of aluminum. Drifter squealed, and the crazed thud of his hooves bashing wood covered the high-pitched screech of a board giving way as its nails were dragged from wood by the force of whatever hit it. Drifter squealed again, this time a long, drawn-out wail of fear.

Danny pawed a leather case about the size of a thin wallet from his back pocket, thumbed it open, and removed a mini-syringe. He dropped the leather case to the floor, used his teeth to separate the plastic cylinder from over the needle, and approached the panicked Quarter Horse's stall. Drifter had swung to face the corner of the stall, and Danny sank the needle fully into the animal's haunch.

Drifter began to rear once again, seemed to think it over for several heartbeats, and then stood gaping dumbly at the vet. Ever so slowly he collapsed onto his bed of straw, slack-jawed, his eyelids fluttering as he struggled to keep them open. The drug was stronger than 1,200 pounds of muscular horseflesh; Drifter's head dropped to the floor as if in slow motion. He snuffed through his nostrils and then slept.

Julie stepped closer to the stall, white faced.

"He's OK now, Julie," Danny assured her. "He'll sleep for a few hours, and by the time he wakes up the storm should be over."

"What about Sunday?" Julie asked. The collie continued panting, and his body trembled like that of a whipped puppy.

"I'm afraid he's going to have to tough it out. The tranquilizer is specifically for horses or cattle. It's too heavy for a canine system. He'll be fine, as long as he can stick close to one or both of us."

Julie returned to her hay bale, sat, and patted her leg. Sunday cringed across the floor to her and huddled between her knees.

Danny walked to the window and gazed outward, although there was nothing to see but a swirl of dirt and darkness.

The voice of the storm—varying from a muted growl to the scream of a circus calliope—was the only constant. The barn groaned under the heavier onslaughts of the wind and during lapses seemed to settle into itself, to gird up for the next battering.

Julie allowed her eyes to close. The last image she focused on before she dozed off was that of Danny standing at the window, his shoulders broad and strong, his right arm raised and his palm flat against the siding next to the window frame. It was a good image, a strong one, the figure of a guardian and a protector.

5

Julie opened her eyes, disoriented. Danny's hand rested on her shoulder as he shook her gently.

"Hey," he said, his voice husky. "Listen—there's no wind. The storm's over."

Julie listened, holding her breath. The silence was like that of the deepest hours of the night. She shuddered.

"It's so quiet it's scary," she said.

"Yeah. You OK? You were kind of murmuring in your sleep, but I didn't want to wake you up." He smiled. "The best way to get past a storm is to sleep through it."

"What time is it?" Julie asked, stretching her arms and working kinks from her neck.

"Quarter to seven," Danny said, glancing at his watch.

"I slept all those hours?" Julie asked incredulously. "What did you do?"

"Well, I gawked out the window for most of the time, just thinking. I checked on Drifter every so often, scratched Sunday, and thought some more. Actually, the time seemed to go quickly. And, speaking of Drifter, let's take a look at him."

Julie stood, brushing at her jeans with little success at re-moving soil or grit, and they stepped to the Quarter Horse's stall. Sunday, back to normal, followed. Drifter, too, was in the process of waking up. His eyes were half closed, and he was coated with a dull veneer of dirt and dust. He hauled his legs under himself and began the clumsy procedure of a horse rising from the ground. When he had all four hooves under him, he shook his entire body like a dog emerging from water. A thick haze rose about him, dense enough to form a brown cloud in his stall. He attempted a step but lurched against the wall.

"He's still a little addled by the tranquilizer," Danny said before Julie could ask a question. "Another hour or so and he'll be as good as new. We'll leave him alone for a bit. C'mon, let's take a look outside."

They walked together to the front of the barn, Julie again slapping ineffectually at the dirt on her shirt and jeans. She put her hand to her hair but took it away quickly when she felt her hair's damp griminess. "I'm a mess," she grumbled.

"Yeah," Danny said, grinning and rubbing his eyes. "I, on the other hand, look like a dewy spring rose."

Julie looked at him and laughed. "What you look like is a destitute raccoon," she said. "The only clean part of you is where you wiped the dirt away from your eyes."

Danny muscled the sliding door open a foot and a half or so. "The track's full of sand. I'll clean it with a cloth and some oil. Do you have a ladder?"

"Just a stepladder, and it's not tall enough."

"That's OK. I've got an extension ladder at home. I'll bring it over and get this done for you."

"Great," Julie said.

Danny looked outside, and Julie, right behind him, peeked over his shoulder. For a long moment, neither spoke as they took in the scene. Sunday eased through the opening and stood in front of the barn, peering around as if he'd never been there before. The light remained murky and made it seem as if they were viewing everything through a soiled window. The air was still in an after-the-storm quietude. It was beyond peaceful—almost frighteningly so, like the silence that shrouds a field after a deadly battle.

"Ohhh," Julie breathed. Danny didn't speak—didn't make a sound.

A drift of what appeared to be very pale sand began at the east end of Julie's house and swept gently upward until it reached her kitchen door, which was hanging from its bottom hinge as if twisted away from its frame by a crazed creature. The mound invaded the house, penetrating the doorway, sloping upward along the inside wall, perhaps three feet high—or four or five beyond where Julie and Danny could see.

The window over the sink stared out at them, shattered, its frame warped away, its very edge resting on the sweep of sand and soil. A plastic trash can Julie had kept outside the kitchen door had been whisked away, and the outdoor thermometer that had been angled outside the kitchen window had been torn away too—taking a foot or so of siding with it. The roof had come through in good stead, and the gutters seemed to be in their normal positions. A trellis at the side of the house was gone, and so were a folding lawn chair and a plastic table.

"It could have been much worse," Danny observed. "Your roof looks fine, and that window is no big deal."

"The roof was new when I bought the house," Julie said. "My lawyer insisted on it, and I thought he was going to blow the deal for me."

"Good lawyer. Roofs are expensive."

Julie nodded. After a moment she said, "Why are we standing out here? Are we afraid to see the inside?"

Danny smiled ruefully. "It'll look worse than it is, Julie. It's a matter of mule-work cleanup, is all. We'll take it a room at a time and, well . . . you'll be back to normal."

Danny stepped out ahead of Julie, and Sunday began to follow him, but Danny waved him back with a sweep of his arm, telling him he was free to explore.

Julie walked behind Danny, hand to her mouth. Her home had been invaded by a force over which she had absolutely no control, and she felt the storm's incursion personally, as if a once-good friend had turned on her for no reason.

A sloping dune of dry soil entered the kitchen and followed the wall, tapering down as it approached the living room. The kitchen and living room were strewn with newspapers and catalogs and junk mail that'd been piled near the door. Julie walked robotically to the stairs, her boots crunching sand and dirt; the sound was loud and abrasive in the quiet house.

She found no dunes or mounds of soil on the second

floor, but everything—her sheets and pillows, her bedside table, her dresser—was coated with a patina of grit, as if the bedroom hadn't been dusted for a very, very long time. The window, open about halfway, had a pool of dirt in front of it that extended across the room like an island in a hardwood sea. Julie's boots continued crunching as she walked to the bathroom. The surfaces—the sink, the toilet-seat cover, the top of the medicine cabinet, and the floor—were painted with grayish-brown dirt. Her Mickey shower curtain offered the only color in the small room, and it seemed frivolous.

Julie didn't realize that Danny was behind her until she felt his hand on her shoulder. "Like I said outside, it could be a lot worse. I've got a Shop-Vac at my place that'll pick all this up."

"That'd be good," she said. "My old Eureka couldn't handle a mess like this. I guess I should sweep first, right? Or shovel, in the kitchen."

"Yeah. That'd be best. I can help you with it."

"How about your place?" Julie asked. "Did you leave any windows open?"

"No sweat. I closed up everything before I left. The clinic will be fine—I've got good windows in it, and the seals are fresh."

"Hey," Julie said, "we've missed a couple of meals. Let me check what I have in the refrigerator. I know I've got some cold cuts and some potato salad."

"Better yet—let's go to the café," Danny said. "If it isn't open, we'll go somewhere else. You need to get out of here for a bit before we tackle the cleanup."

113

"Sounds good, but look at me—at us. We're walking dirt piles."

"Sure we are—and so is everyone else within a hundred or so miles. We know everybody at the café, and they know us. It'll be like it was after that Thanksgiving blizzard. As soon as people could get out and around, they headed to Drago's."

"I don't know, Danny . . ." Julie slapped at her jeans, putting a brown cloud of dust in the air from each leg.

"C'mon," he said, taking her hand. "The only thing we have to worry about are the cats . . ."

Julie walked a couple of steps with him and then stopped, turning to face him. "Cats? Why do we need to worry about cats?"

Danny grinned, his teeth very white against the soil on his face. "They'll think we're walking litter boxes."

Danny's truck protested a bit as he cranked the engine. He climbed out, leaving Julie in the passenger seat and Sunday at her feet—in fact, on her feet. Danny opened the hood, unscrewed the cover over the air filter to the fuel-injection system, and removed the paper mesh filter. He flapped it in the air, and Julie watched through the windshield as the filter changed in color from a drab ecru to a dull eggshell. He reassembled the parts and slammed the hood. When he settled behind the wheel he smiled at Julie and turned the key. The engine growled to life, hesitated once, leveled out, and then purred smoothly.

"My hero."

"You betcha," Danny said.

Julie reached over and squeezed his arm as he drove down the driveway. Danny closed his hand over hers for a moment and then removed it to shift into second gear as they reached the road.

The heat had returned, seemingly with new strength and new vehemence. Danny clicked on the air-conditioning, and the vents spewed dirt into the cab. "Bad idea," he said, turning off the air. Julie sneezed, and so did Sunday. Danny pressed the window button and lowered his and Julie's windows.

Julie felt like she was riding on a road she didn't know, in a place she'd never visited. Tumbleweeds littered the roadway, some enmeshed in fences, most resting where the wind had dropped them when the storm died. Some were sizable—a yard and more across—and countless more were close to that size. Danny slowed and downshifted back to first gear as he eased through a mass of them that'd collected on the road and shoulder where a scraggly stand of ponderosa pine had long ago taken root. The truck seemed to push through the gathering of tumbleweeds without actually touching them, as if the mere motion of the air in front of the vehicle was enough to ease them to the sides.

Ahead, at the center of a long curve, a spit of dirt reached halfway across the road. Julie noticed a glint of metal. "Danny, what's that?" she asked, leaning forward against her shoulder harness. As they drew closer, the object became more visible: a rural mailbox with part of its wooden mounting post still

115

attached to it. Although the box was partially crumpled and more than a bit twisted, the letters "DUN" were still readable in scratched but vivid red hand-painted script.

"That's the Duncans' mailbox," Julie said. "But it can't be—they live better than five miles from here."

Danny pulled closer to the shoulder, stopped, shifted to neutral, and flicked on his four-way warning flashers. "Probably more than five miles, but look there." He pointed across a barren field that seemed to stretch to the far horizon. "That should've been a few hundred acres of better'n knee-high barley and oats. But there's next to nothing to stop that mailbox from blowing all this way." He got out of the truck and walked to the box. He attempted to wrench its front open, but the distorted aluminum wouldn't allow him to do so. Danny carried it back and set it down behind his seat. "There's something in it. I'll drop by the Duncan farm tomorrow." He sat with his hands on the wheel but didn't move to start the engine.

"What?" Julie asked quietly.

"I'm worried about these people."

For a moment, Julie wasn't at all sure whom Danny was referring to. "You mean the Duncan family?"

Danny laughed quietly. "No, not the Duncans—I mean the Duncans and everyone else in this part of the state, I guess. At times when I've been driving, I'll pull off to the side of the road and try to remember how the land looked when it was green and healthy, like it's supposed to be. And I can't really remember. I can see images in my mind of crops and fields of corn and so forth, but as to actually remembering the smells and the tactile stuff—how it feels to walk through a good, lush pasture with the grass almost knee high—it seems like it never happened. It's as if those times were something I hallucinated or imagined and what we have now is the way it's always been." He laughed again, this time self-consciously. "I must sound like a wacko, right?"

"No—no, you don't. I've had feelings like that too. I keep wondering how long all this can last, how long people can stand it, before they simply give up. It makes me sad."

"Yeah." Danny was silent for a moment. He reached over and took Julie's hand, and she grasped his willingly, comfortably.

"We haven't seen anything like this in our country in the time we've been alive," Danny said. "The thing is, history shows us that disasters have happened before—droughts, flooding, disease, wars, all that. I have to believe that there's something in the American people—in us and the people around us—that helps us survive. Maybe it's love of God, maybe it's that we love our country so much—but we always survive and come back stronger."

Julie realized that she was hearing Danny Pulver's heart speaking directly to her. She wanted him to continue speaking, to continue sharing, to let her know more about him and what made him the man he was.

Sunday snuffled in his sleep, shifted his position on the floor in front of Julie, and dozed again.

"What I'm the most worried about are the families—the families of the farmers and of the businesspeople too," Danny said. "It's a tragedy to lose a farm or a business, the kind of tragedy that can tear at the heart of a family. Remember I was whining about my practice? I feel like a jerk for saying what I did. My obligations will be taken care of, sooner or later. As quickly as I can pay them, I will. I can't do any more than that. But I ache inside when I think how a farm family feels when they look out over acres and acres of dust and know that any day the bank's going to put a notice on their door. Or when I think about a family closing the door for the last time on their small business that failed."

"I guess all we can do is keep on keeping on," Julie said. "I know that sounds silly and lightweight, but I think it's the basic thing about our people—they never give up, and they keep on keeping on, no matter how difficult it is."

Danny nodded and turned to face her. The air was completely still, and not even the call of a night bird broke the silence. Their eyes met, and Danny put his arm around her shoulders and pulled her toward him. For a long moment, Julie didn't speak—neither of them spoke.

"Danny?" she finally said, her voice husky and strained.

"Mmm?"

"My shoulder harness," she choked out. "It's strangling me."

Danny released her immediately, a stricken look on his face. Their eyes met again as Julie settled back in her seat and took a deep breath. She was the first to giggle, but Danny joined her in a heartbeat. Then they were both laughing—heartily, uproariously, much harder than the event really deserved. But it was the unexpected joy of relief, of quick giddiness amidst difficulty, and it felt very good to Julie.

Sunday rearranged himself in front of Julie and poked her with his snout. She leaned forward. "We can't leave Sunny out of a hug," she said.

Danny leaned awkwardly toward Julie and the collie, reaching for them with his arms. "No—we can't," he said.

The rest of the ride to Coldwater was uneventful, and Julie and Danny were comfortable in the silence.

Danny is opening up to me—finally. He let me inside his defenses, and what a sweet and sensitive man I found there. She glanced over at him. *There may be something here for both of us,* she thought. Strangely, her mind flashed a picture of the cop, Ken Townsend. The image vaguely disturbed her—perhaps irritated her—and she chased it away by concentrating on Danny.

A dozen or more pickups, cars, and a couple of SUVs were pulled to the long curb that fronted Drago's on Main Street. The street itself was littered with the detritus of the storm. A large sheet of plywood hung from the few nails that still held it to the frame of the front window of a defunct book and music store. The tumbleweeds had found their way to Coldwater as well and were as ubiquitous as pedestrians and shoppers used to be. One scudded by, broomed along by the breeze that had just arisen, as Danny, Julie, and Sunday climbed out of the truck. They watched it until it stopped against the rear wheel of an old Chevrolet Blazer.

Danny left the collie out in front on the sidewalk with a stay command. The front door to Drago's was cracked vertically for almost its full length. Duct tape had been applied from the inside. The aroma of broiling hamburgers, onions, and strong coffee filled the diner. Julie took a booth and waved to a few friends, while Danny waited at the counter. He asked for three raw burgers and a soup bowl of cold water. When his order had been filled he took the paper plate and the water back outside to his dog, crouched, scratched Sunday for a moment, and returned to the restaurant. He ordered three hamburgers—cooked, this time—two plates of French fries, two coffees, an order of onion rings, and two large soft drinks.

Danny had been right about the attire and degree of cleanliness of the patrons at the diner, Julie noticed. Men and women were grubby, sweaty, and tired. They slouched in their chairs and in the booths like weary soldiers after a long, hard march. The level of conversation was subdued, but every so often short bursts of laughter rang out, and the person laughing invariably looked embarrassed when Julie's eyes found him or her.

She watched Danny standing at the counter as he waited for their order. With this much of a crowd it was quicker to wait at the counter than to wait for a harried waitress to make the trip to a booth or table.

A complex man—and a good man. But in the past it's always seemed like something was holding him back from becoming really close. Am I certain that there's no one else in his life, no other romantic interest?

"Hey, Julie—I see you survived the storm."

Julie pulled her gaze away from Danny, slightly flustered

for a moment. Ken Townsend stood at the booth, looking down at her, his teeth white against the tan of his face. He was dressed in jeans, boots, and a sleeveless sweatshirt with a washed-out picture of Daffy Duck on its front.

"I imagine you've been busy today, Ken," she said.

He nodded. "May I?" He motioned to the bench seat across from Julie.

"Sure. I'm with Danny Pulver—he's getting our food. Do you know him?"

"I know the name, but we haven't met yet. He's the vet, right? He owns that beautiful collie I saw outside?"

"That's Danny," Julie said. "So—were you really busy?"

"Yeah—patrolling, mostly, and some traffic control earlier. Nothing I could do about the storm except be around when people needed me. I saw lots of damage to houses and barns, stuff like that. There's been no injuries to anyone so far, though, and I'm grateful for that. Some of the McKee cattle were roaming, but Sam and his boys went out on horseback and rounded them up. Either a section of fence blew down or the cattle panicked and rammed it, Sam said." He sighed. "I finished my regular shift and then cruised on my own, seeing if anyone needed help with anything. I guess the worst is over. Now it's just a matter of putting things back together."

Julie looked at Ken as he sat down. So, she noticed, were the women and young girls who were in any proximity to the booth.

Danny walked up, balancing a plastic tray piled with food and drinks. Julie smiled and shifted close to the wall to give him room to sit next to her. "Do you know Ken Townsend, Danny?" she asked.

Danny set the tray on the table and extended his hand. "Danny Pulver," he said. "Good to meet you, Ken." The two men shook hands. "Going to eat with us?"

"I'd love to—I'm starved." Then, Ken seemed to reconsider. "Unless I'd be . . . ?"

Danny waved away Ken's question. "A guy's gotta eat, right? Anyway, I've seen you wheeling around in that rocket the PD gave you. It's a 427, isn't it?"

Ken smiled proudly. "Five-speed, heavy-duty clutch, handling package, channeled exhausts, zero to eighty in about seven seconds—the whole smash."

"Wow," Danny breathed. "What's the top end?"

"I'll tell you this," Ken said with a grin. "The police speedometer stops at 140. The tachometer doesn't stop anywhere. I'd estimate about a hundred and a half flat out in fifth gear. There's lots of long, empty roads around here . . ."

Danny nodded as if he and Ken were partners agreeing on something that influenced them both.

"Gee, this sure is interesting," Julie said and then faked a yawn.

Danny and Ken glanced at one another and broke out in laughter. "Sorry, Julie," Danny said, "but I was a gearhead through high school, and cars like Ken's have always fascinated me."

"Sorry, Julie—I got carried away too, I guess," Ken said.

"I was only teasing," Julie assured him.

"How did your places come through the storm?" Ken asked.

"I had a little damage but nothing major,"Julie said. "Now I've got a desert in my house. I ran out to the barn without shutting the windows—or the kitchen door. It's kind of a mess."

"After we eat we're going to clean it up,"Danny said. "I've got a Shop-Vac that'll do most of the work."

"Need another strong back?" Ken offered. "I'm off duty and don't have a thing to do. I'd love to help out."

"Oh, Ken—that's not necessary."

"Umm . . . many hands make work light and all that," Danny said. "Thanks for the offer."

Ken shoved out of the booth. "I'll get some burgers and chow down with you, then. Anyone need anything else from the counter?"

Danny and Julie shook their heads, since they'd both taken bites of their hamburgers. Danny swallowed and took a sip of soft drink. "Ken seems like a nice guy," he said.

Julie nodded. "He is. I think he's a good cop too. He was out cruising after he finished his shift, he told me, looking for anyone who needed help."

"Does he have family here?" Danny asked.

"No—when I interviewed him he told me he was single. He was a private investigator in Billings for several years before joining up with the Coldwater PD."

"Those PIs have always fascinated me, just like fast cars," Danny said, picking up a french fry. "It'll be interesting to talk to him about that."

Ken came back and took his seat across from Danny and Julie. His tray held two hamburgers, two orders of French fries, and a pair of large coffees in Styrofoam cups.

They ate in companionable silence, listening to the muted buzz of conversation around them as more people dropped by the café. Finally, they sat finishing their drinks.

"Time to get to it?" Ken asked.

"Might just as well," Danny said. "We're going to stop and pick up my vacuum." He looked at Julie. "How about giving Ken directions to your place?"

"I know where it is," Ken said.

Danny's and Julie's eyes met for a second, and then Danny looked back at his coffee cup. "Great. See you there, then."

Julie settled against the passenger door, Sunday at her feet in his usual riding position. Danny drove carefully, using his high beams as his eyes swept the road for things dropped by the storm.

"I didn't realize how hungry I was," she said. "I just about inhaled my hamburger."

"Me too," Danny agreed.

Julie reflected on the meal and the conversation, her eyes following the cones of light cast by the headlamps. She smiled to herself. *I was the queen of the café with those two guys hovering around me. There wasn't a woman in the place who wasn't checking out our booth.* Julie admitted to herself that the attention—the admiration—felt pretty good.

Danny and Ken seemed to take to one another right away. I'd like them to be friends. And it's so nice of Ken to offer to pitch in with the cleanup. I wonder what he's up to? Just bored or maybe a little lonely? Maybe interested in me as a friend—or more? The candy bars and now helping out at home . . .

Just hold your horses, she chided herself. *Ken wants to fit into Coldwater. And he has no family and doesn't know a whole lot of people here. He's just being friendly.*

"I won't be a minute," Danny said as he pulled to a stop next to his home. "The vac's in the shed." He opened his door and stepped out of the truck. Sunday bounded out after him. "I'm going to leave Sunny here, I think," Danny said. "He'll be in the way at your place."

Julie opened her door and walked over to the barn, where Danny's Appaloosa, Dakota, was standing. Dakota leaned his neck over his stall, and Julie stroked him. "Yuck," she said. His coat was thick with loose dirt. "Been rolling since the storm, hey, Dakota?"

She heard the slam of the back door of the truck. "Ready, Julie?" Danny called. She gave a final scratch to the horse's muzzle and turned back to the truck.

Cleaning great quantities of fine dust and dirt from inside the house was a formidable task. Even if a section of hardwood floor appeared clean, walking over it in boots resulted in a grinding, crackling sound that Danny, Julie, and Ken quickly learned to hate.

The shovel and bucket labor in the kitchen and the hallway came first. At first they were trying to work too fast and as a consequence were getting in one another's way. After Ken had inadvertently speared Danny in the stomach with the end of his shovel, they decided that Julie should take her bedroom and leave the kitchen, at least, to the men. With one person fewer in the room, the mound diminished quickly.

Julie ran the Shop-Vac in her bedroom, amazed at the strength of the suction the machine offered. But as she walked across an expanse of floor that looked bare and clean, she crunched on a minute layer of grit left behind. She sighed, ran the back of her hand across her forehead, and clicked on the vac once again. The roar of the vacuum and the mindless repetition of the work insulated her from the rest of the world as she cleaned. When she turned off the vacuum twenty minutes later, her shirt was almost sopping wet with sweat and her lower back was burning. She plopped down heavily on her bed and sat on its edge. From downstairs bits of the conversation between Ken and Danny reached her. She listened with half a mind until she caught the name Maggie.

". . . a really great lady," Danny's voice said. "But it didn't work out. She married Ian Lane, the minister here."

"That's too bad," Ken said. After a moment, he added, "I had a similar thing back in Billings a few years ago. Linda was her name. It just didn't work out." There was another pause. "I would've married her in a second."

"Yeah. I know what you mean." Danny's voice didn't sound particularly sad, but there was weight to the statement that seemed more important than the sum of the words.

Julie listened to the shovels scraping the linoleum and

the *shh* sound of soil being dumped into buckets. The right thing to do would be to turn on the vacuum cleaner and get back to work, she realized. Listening to a conversation she wasn't a part of was bad manners, a sort of duplicity that Julie disliked in others—and in herself. Nevertheless, she made no move from where she sat.

"I guess things usually work out for the best," Ken said.

"You don't sound like you believe that."

"Sometimes I do, sometimes I don't. I was kinda shocked when Linda and I broke up, but moping gets old, you know?"

"Mmm," Danny responded noncommittally.

The men worked, grunting occasionally, as they lifted full shovels. They'd apparently staggered their times going out the door to dump their buckets near the barn in order to avoid walking into one another.

"Have you been seeing Julie long?" Ken asked.

"Not real long, no." Danny's answer wasn't terse exactly, but it had a different sound that hadn't been present before.

"Hey—I didn't mean to—"

Danny's laugh sounded forced to Julie. "Forget it. How about telling me about your PI work?" The rapid change of subject was apparently welcome to both men.

"Surveillance, Danny—that's the entire job description. I've spent more hours sitting in my car trying to stay awake and alert than I can count. One time I was watching a guy who'd ripped off the firm he worked for . . ."

Julie stood and walked to the vacuum. Again, its roar separated her from the world but not from her thoughts.

"Not real long, no." What did he mean by that? Haven't we been friends for over a year? Almost two years? Maybe that's not really seeing one another . . . but still . . . An uninvited and unwanted headline appeared in Julie's consciousness:

Devious, Snooping Reporter Gets Just What She Deserves

Ken and Danny, finally finished with the kitchen, moved their operations into the living room. The dirt and dust hadn't accumulated as heavily in there, and the cleanup consisted of thorough dusting, gathering loose papers that had been blown about, and vacuuming the carpet.

Julie, satisfied with her bedroom after walking across its wonderfully crunch-free floor, moved on to the bathroom after giving up the vac to the men.

Ultimately the cleaning crew—tired, grimy, and sweaty but triumphant—met at the kitchen table. Julie passed out cans of soda and sank into a chair. "I just checked on Drifter again," she said. "He's fine. Alert, scrounging for an apple. He's as good as new."

"I looked in on him a few times too, when I was out emptying my bucket," Danny said. "He's happy as can be—all the attention he's getting."

Julie looked around the kitchen. "You guys are wonderful. I don't know how to thank you. It would've taken me forever to clean up this mess."

"No big deal," Ken said. He smiled. "Although I'll tell you what—next storm, lock the place down, OK?"

"Absolutely. I promise."

"Your kitchen window looks like a standard size," Danny said. "The frame is shot, but they're sold as a unit. I'll pick one up at the hardware store and put it in for you. And I'll clean and oil the track on the barn door too."

"Terrific. Just charge the window to my name, and I'll stop by and pay for it."

"Anything else I can help with?" Ken asked.

"Not a thing—but again, thanks. I really appreciate all you've done."

"I actually kind of enjoyed it. Plus, Danny and I got to talk a little. I'm glad I decided to stop at the café."

"So are we," Danny said.

"I have an idea," Julie said. "How about if next Wednesday I broil some steaks and make a fancy meal for my two heroes? Kind of a thank-you dinner. What do you think?"

"You've talked me into it. What can I bring?" Ken asked.

"Nothing—just yourself. About 7:00? Danny?"

"Sounds great to me. Sure—7:00 on Wednesday is fine."

Julie watched as Ken in the Ford cruiser followed Danny's truck down the driveway to the road. When their taillights disappeared in the darkness she went into her now-clean home. Then came a moment she'd thought about longingly throughout the afternoon and night.

The shower was wonderful.

6

Sunday morning wake-up came very quickly for Julie. It had been well after 3:00 a.m. when she collapsed into the fresh sheets she'd put on her bed—and her alarm seemed to go off within seconds of closing her eyes. Even though she was in good shape, and the riding and barn work kept excess pounds away, her body ached as if she'd played a full game with the National Football League.

As she walked into the barn, Drifter snorted as if chastising her for leaving him in his stall overly long. She led him across the aisle to a fresh stall, filled his grain bin and water bucket, and tossed a flake of hay to him. Her manure fork seemed to weigh as much as a telephone pole, and the wheelbarrow had somehow gained weight overnight, but she felt good when her chores were finished.

Julie showered again, but this second shower wasn't the extravaganza of cleaning and scrubbing of the night before. Yesterday's clothes rested in a heap on the bathroom floor, and she left them there yet again, promising to do her laundry later. Fortunately, her bedroom closet door had been closed during the storm; all she needed to do was shake out the skirt and blouse she selected for church.

Services at the Coldwater Church were held at 9:30 and 11:30 on Sundays. The most heavily attended was the early service, and many of the ranchers and farmers considered even that hour to be terribly late.

Julie pulled into the parking lot and noticed that there were fewer cars and trucks than normal. The congregation was generally a happy one, friendly and open, but this day many of the people Julie saw looked frazzled, obviously tired and worn out. The temperature had reached ninety-three degrees by 8:30, she knew from her truck radio. The sun seemed to be maliciously focused on the frame building of the church, and although the stained glass windows filtered the brassy sunlight, the air inside was heavy.

Still, the peace of the place seemed to raise spirits a bit. The light buzz of conversation during the pre-service time was that of people sharing—and somehow lightening—their difficulties. Hushed laughter occurred sporadically, and it sounded good to Julie.

These are strong people, she thought. *It'll take more than a drought to step on their spirit.*

Cyrus, Wylie, James, and Otis Huller were seated in their usual pew, about midway to the altar. Each wore a navy blue suit, a stiffly starched white shirt, and a somber, almost funereal, dark tie. The family sat arranged from oldest to youngest with Cyrus, the patriarch, at the aisle, staring straight ahead. The men sat as still as a line of meticulously arranged toy soldiers.

Julie remembered that Sunday almost three years ago when the Hullers had a flat tire in their old station wagon and were late to service. A family—a young business owner, his wife, and their three young children—had settled into the Huller's customary pew. Cyrus stood in the aisle, his sons in perfect single file behind him, and glared at the young man. At first the young fellow didn't want to move—there were, after all, other pews open. But he and his family were new to the church, and his wife was red faced and elbowing him, and the old man's eyes were like searchlights focused on him. So he got up and moved his family, and that was the last time anyone tried to usurp the Huller pew at the 9:30 service.

Ian Lane had talked to old Cyrus a few days after the incident, Maggie had told Julie. "You know, Cyrus, we don't have assigned pews at Coldwater Church. Those folks had every right to be where they were."

Huller considered that for a moment and then said, "That's where me an' my boys always sit at church." He turned away, ending the conversation.

Julie stopped next to Cyrus Huller and touched his shoulder. "Hi, Mr. Huller—Julie Downs. I called you a few days ago about an interview. OK if I stop by your farm this afternoon to talk?"

The old gentleman cleared his throat. He rarely spoke in church, and when he did, he used the same loud, no-nonsense voice he used elsewhere. "Like I said when you called, I don't know that I got much to tell you, but sure. You stop on by. Ain't much else to do around home lately. I'd just as soon jaw with a pretty lady as not."

Julie's face reddened as heads turned toward her and Mr. Huller. She settled into the next pew. She looked around the church, trying to appear as casual as possible.

This Sunday Rev. Lane talked about the storm and the drought and how his congregation was being tried by the conditions around them. Then he paused for a long moment and shifted gears precipitously. A smile played on his lips.

"One of our farmers and his wife were out looking at the sky," Ian told the congregation. "The wife said, 'Look, honey—rain clouds!'

"The farmer looked at the sky more closely. 'Nah,' he said. 'Those aren't rain clouds—they're just empties coming back from somewhere else.'"

A rather profound silence settled over the room. Then, chuckles erupted from various parts of the congregation—which led to more chuckles and then to laughter.

There was a perceptible stirring inside the church, as if the congregation was awakening from a light doze. A silly joke delivered at a dark moment wouldn't change the situations the people faced, but it lightened the burden they carried for a moment.

The sermon—and some of those present weren't quite sure that it actually was a sermon—was short. Rev. Lane talked about the bits of joy that are always present in life if people look for them. When he concluded with a prayer, there were more smiles in the group than worry-creased foreheads.

The fellowship hour following the service wasn't well attended. Most of the church members still had storm cleanup work to do. Julie and Maggie stood near the long table that held juice, coffee, bagels, and sweet rolls and discussed the storm.

"So," Maggie said after telling her own cleanup tale, "what's on your schedule today?"

"I'm going to run the vacuum over to Danny, and then I'm going to talk with Cyrus Huller for a story I've got planned. Kind of a historical perspective piece."

"Sounds interesting. He's a crusty ol' fellow, though. Think he'll give you much of what you need?"

Julie smiled. "I can be kind of crusty myself, when I have to be. Anyway, he agreed to talk with me, so I'll see what happens."

A pair of teens stepped up to talk with Maggie, and Julie tossed her empty Styrofoam cup into a trash basket and drifted toward the door. As she walked across the parking lot to her truck, the asphalt surface radiated heat in shimmering curtains that reminded her once again that whatever problems she was having in her life, the drought remained the biggest concern for all those who were living under its oppression.

Julie was glad that she hadn't changed out of the clothes she'd worn to church that morning when she pulled in next to the Huller's truck and glanced at the front porch of the one-hundred-year-old home in which the father and three sons lived. Cyrus was in his Sunday clothes, tie snug, sitting in a rocking chair. Next to him was a small table with a pitcher of iced tea. One glass was in his hand, the other waiting for Julie.

Three hounds, each a long, long way from puppyhood, dragged themselves out from under the porch, bayed a couple of times without much enthusiasm at Julie, and then walked over to her, tails beginning to wag.

"Get on away from the lady, ya useless fleabags!" Cyrus called out. The animals paid no attention to him. Julie rubbed and scratched each old dog for a moment and then climbed the few stairs to the porch.

"Thanks for seeing me, Mr. Huller. I appreciate it. As I mentioned, what I'm trying to do is put a story together that kind of compares and contrasts what you've seen in the past with what's going on now. I'm not at all sure my readers—the younger ones, anyhow—know much about the Great Depression of the 1930s. I've researched the time and found out how hard things were with drought and dust storms and people's farms being foreclosed on by banks, and how a crop wouldn't bring even the money it cost to grow it. I reread John Steinbeck's *The Grapes of Wrath* too. I wanted to at least understand the basics when we talked."

"Yeah. Well, the thing is that my stories are old an' tired, Miss Julie. I'm not any John Steinbeck either. My stories are things that most folks—if they aren't in the ground already—wanna forget about."

Julie reached for her glass of iced tea, took a long drink, and put it down on the table. "Aren't we seeing the same thing now?" she asked.

Cyrus settled back in his chair. "No," he said quite strongly.

136

He locked eyes with her, and his gaze was close to a glare. "Your research wasn't like being there and living it."

Julie stopped her rocker so she could stare directly into the old man's eyes. "I know a little about the Dust Bowl, at least from books. You're right—I didn't live through it, but you did, sir. That's why I'm here."

Huller thought about that for a moment. "Feisty, ain't you?"

"I don't know about that. I'm just asking you to tell me what you remember so that I can turn it into a story for the *News-Express*."

"I had a girlfriend once who was feisty," Cyrus said. "You kinda remind me of her."

"I'll take that as a compliment," Julie said, smiling.

"That's how I meant it. All right, let's talk."

Julie settled more comfortably in her rocker. "How about starting with what's happening around here, Mr. Huller—on your farm?"

Cyrus waved his arm, taking in the barns and acres that spread out before them. Julie heard the man's stiffly starched shirt rub against his arm as he made the sweeping motion.

"Looks like me an' the boys are gonna lose a good part of our land. We borrowed heavy against it, got us a new combine, new tractor, some other things." He paused. "You have any idea what a new combine big enough for this place costs, Miss Julie?"

"No, I don't."

"Not many people do 'cept the folks who sell them and

137

those who buy them. I got almost a million dollars worth of machinery and nothin' to harvest with it. Nothin'. Couple thousand acres of brush, tumbleweeds, and dead corn spikes."

Julie nodded but said nothing. Mr. Huller was staring off at his main barn, his head moving slowly side to side.

"You ever hear 'bout Black Sunday, Miss Julie?"

"You mean the stock market crash? Back in 1929, when—"

"That was Black Thursday," Cyrus interrupted. "Black Sunday, you see, happened in '35, all 'cross Oklahoma. I was eight years old, but I remember that day. First thing that happened was this huge swarm of birds, all kinds of birds, was flyin' hard as they could to the east. The cloud of birds filled the sky like a huge black front movin' in on us, and the racket they made, why, it hurt a person's ears. You never heard such a thing, this high-pitched shriek that didn't sound at all like birds should sound. And lots of them was droppin' outta the sky like rain, thunkin' down on our roof an' fields an' everywhere. Scared me real bad. Scared my ma and sister too."

Huller poured more iced tea into Julie's glass and topped off his own. "We had to shovel those birds up into baskets an' bury them afterward. What was happening was that the poor birds was tryin' to outfly the storm that was so big and carried so much soil in it that it blocked out the sun and turned that nice, sunny Sunday dark as night. My ma, she hauled me and my brothers and sisters down into the root cellar, and we listened to the wind howl an' glass break an' what sounded like big steam locomotives racin' by.

My ma thought maybe it was the end of the world, an' we all prayed that day, down there in the dark. We'd clapped the big doors shut, and they were good, tight doors my pa built, but the wind just found every little crack an' opening, and there was a mist of dirt in the air down in that little cellar, and we all took to coughin' an' gaspin', an' Ma ripped pieces outta our shirts an' her dress to put over our mouths and noses. My littlest sister never did get over it. She died before she was sixteen, wheezin' an' chokin' for breath, jus' like a winded horse."

"I'm so sorry, Mr. Huller," Julie said. After a minute passed, she asked, "Where was your father, sir?"

"He'd gone off the Friday before to Toole City—'bout eighty miles away—to see if he could borrow some money from the bank there. See, the crop was already gone for the year, choked out by the drought that'd settled in 1932 an' 1933. Pa didn't get back until the Tuesday after Black Sunday. I recall he had tears all down his face when he finally rode up to the house. There was waves of soil alongside the barn and in the fields an' across the roads. Wasn't really soil, though. It was more like powder—all gritty an' dry."

Julie attempted to speak and found her mouth too dry to form words. She took a long drink of her tepid iced tea. "How did people react?"

The old man snorted. "React? Just like they always do, I guess. Some got angry an' took it out on their animals or their families, some jus' plain gave up, an' some made some money from it. I guess most of us, though, lived with it and did the best we could. It was then that all the flyers about

139

the easy work an' good money in California started showin' up. An what was called labor contractors too, who promised good work and nice homes to folks who'd go to California an' pick fruit an' vegetables. These contractors would charge whatever they could gouge outta a family an' send 'em off on a train to California." He paused. "Wasn't any work there that paid enough to feed a man an' his family—none at all. Even with whole families pickin' all day long, dawn to dark. A man'd be lucky to walk off with a whole dollar at the end of the day."

"What did your family do?" Julie asked.

"Well, we lasted a couple more months. We sold or slaughtered the cattle we had, an' the pigs an' chickens too. Pa wrote to his cousin here in Montana. Jeremy Shiftler was his name. Ma called him Jeremy Shiftless, 'cause he was a lazy no-account who'd lucked into a bunch of land—this farm—his folks left him. Jeremy didn't know nor care any more about farming than a duck does, but Pa, he made the place make money. We were lucky, Miss Julie. Finally, Pa bought the farm from Jeremy an', well, here we are. Like I said, we were awful lucky."

"But now this," Julie said quietly.

"Thing is, I seen this once in my life. Seems like that'd be enough for a man. Havin' to sell off parts of my land kinda tears the heart right outta me. I always planned to leave the farm to my boys intact, just like I got it." His voice trailed off.

"But you lived through it, Mr. Huller. You and your sons

have a wonderful farm here—even if you have to sell some acreage . . ."

"Isn't any 'if' about it. You're right about the farm. It's been real good to us. But I'll be long in the ground by the time anything worth harvestin' comes out of it again, I guess."

Julie felt the old man's weariness. "One more thing, Mr. Huller," she said, standing up from her rocker. "What can I tell my readers about how to get through this? What advice can you give them?"

The old man stood too. Julie offered him her right hand, and he took it slowly, as if he wasn't quite sure about this woman shaking hands like a man. In Julie's palm Huller's hand was hard with years of calluses, and very dry, but quite gentle against her own.

"Hope is about all I can say. That an' pray. I don't know that we have any more options than that, Miss Julie. But I'll tell you what—after we sell off a piece we'll have more land left than most families have. We're grateful for that."

Julie smiled at him and said good-bye. As she eased down the driveway in her truck, Otis Huller rode across a field that should have been tall and green with corn. He sat atop a fancy bay mare with the grace of a longtime horseman. Julie stopped and lowered her window.

"Hi, Julie. You and Pa have a good talk?" He slid down from the Quarter Horse, reins in his left hand. Julie looked up at him. Otis, shaggy-haired and muscular with a flinty face and a tan so deep that he could never lose it, met her gaze.

"I learned a lot from him, and I feel for him."

"He's seen some hard times," Otis said. "I think he's tired. Not physically—the man's still a bull, no doubt about that. He's a little tired in spirit is what I mean. He doesn't want to fight with the heat and the drought and the crops."

"Is it possible that he's not going to farm anymore?"

A smile spread slowly across Otis's face; his teeth were straight and almost startlingly white against the darkness of his skin. "Nope. That's not possible. And I'll tell you what, Julie—my pa will quit farming on the same day Lulu here"—he nodded toward his mare—"learns to play the fiddle. My pa has more Montana soil in his veins than he does blood. He's down, is all, but he isn't a quitter, no matter what. There aren't any quitters in the Huller family—there never were and never will be."

Julie smiled at Otis. "I guess I knew that."

She had her story.

7

Julie smiled as her fingers moved over the keyboard. She wasn't fast—barely a touch typist with perhaps too many peeks at the keys—but the words seemed to flow from her heart through her fingers this evening. At times, in previous stories, she'd had to dredge words and images from their hiding places somewhere inside herself, but the Huller story and its broader message of hope flowed as smoothly as cream from a pitcher.

She pushed back her chair from her desk and let her shoulders sag. A glance at the clock surprised her; she'd been working nonstop for over four hours, yet her mind was still clicking, and sentences seemed to appear on her monitor almost on their own. She picked up the pages she'd printed out with the photos scanned into them. The story headline was bold and stark, juxtaposing its powerful statement, "No Quitters in This Family," with a picture of the dead and dying corn spikes.

Mr. Huller's history of Black Sunday and the other events that had taken place in Oklahoma during the course of his childhood was just that—history. But even more than that, it was proof that families could and did prevail against drought

143

and crop failure even more dire than the drought strangling Montana now. "We're having hard times," Julie's article said between its lines, "but we'll beat this thing."

She reread her pages and determined that the final word count was 2,291, slightly over her space allocation, which allowed for some editing by in-house staff. Julie placed the pages and the originals of the photos—along with Cyrus Huller's permission to quote—in a file folder.

The walls of her office seemed to draw in on her now, and her throat was parched and dry. She took a deep breath, feeling a nagging ache in her shoulders and a burgeoning throbbing at her temples. She felt like she'd just plowed forty acres of rocky land.

The fatigue was a good feeling in a way—the sensation of a job well done. Still, Julie knew that if she didn't get outside her office and her house, she'd scream. She shut down her computer and hustled down the stairs, boots only grinding on missed grit a few times as she left her home and stood outside her kitchen door.

The night was clear, and the stars seemed more multitudinous than usual. Although the temperature was a couple degrees over ninety, the unfathomable depth of the sky and the spectacular glinting of the stars offered a grand respite from Julie's little workplace.

She found it easy to imagine that she was alone on the earth—the only human on the entire planet. The only sounds that reached her were the occasional high-pitched squeak of a bat and the whir of insects that her boots stirred out of the desiccated pasture grass.

Julie meandered toward the few trees that Drifter favored during the heat of the day. The adrenaline rush of completing the story seemed to drain from her like air from a punctured balloon as she walked across the pasture. Her mind began the inevitable second-guessing that seemed to be an unwelcome part of every writer's toolbox.

Did I twist the story too hard? Did I misuse what Mr. Huller was actually saying in order to focus the story more positively? Was what Otis said to me as important as I indicated it was? Could what Mr. Huller said be seen as a statement that leaving Coldwater is the only way to beat the drought?

Julie sat on the ground and leaned her back against one of the trees. She wiped perspiration from her forehead and realized what a habitual gesture this was. She scratched up some dry dirt with a fingernail and then let the dirt fall from her palm back to the ground. The soil held no more moisture than desert sand. She scraped more soil, this time digging deeper, using all of her fingers, and dug out a handful of what felt like salt in her palm. She tossed the dirt into the air and watched it sift down in the moonlight.

Out on the road adjacent to her pasture a car powered through a gentle curve, its exhaust rapping powerfully as it accelerated. Suddenly, Ken Townsend was in her mind, and she found herself smiling.

Sleep was ragged that night, filled with images of Danny and Ken and her story. Julie threw the sheet aside twenty minutes before her alarm was set to go off at 5:45, swung her feet out of bed and to the floor, and sat up. Her night-gown was sticking to her, and she sat with her palms against her temples as if trying to squeeze away the dull throb of a headache. She pulled on jeans and a T-shirt, stopped to drink directly from the carton of orange juice in her refrigerator, and put on a pot of coffee to brew. She glanced at the thermometer outside her kitchen window and groaned aloud: eighty-four degrees.

Her barn chores went quickly. She applied the salve to Drifter's scratches and fed him his morning ration of grain and fresh hay. She moved mechanically, forking soiled straw into her wheelbarrow, humming a little tune, talking to Drifter. When her work was finished and she'd turned the horse out to pasture, she put her pitchfork and wheelbarrow away and stood at the fence to watch Drifter as he meandered toward the stand of trees. As if he knew he was being observed, he picked up his pace to a smart jog, his tail flowing behind him, his body working effortlessly as it covered ground. Julie was smiling as she returned to her home.

When she came out of her house an hour later, fresh from a quick shower and invigorated by a couple cups of coffee and a bowl of cereal, she stopped a few feet from her truck and looked at it with a critical eye. It was a mess, as dusty and dirty as it would have been if it had sat in a barn for a generation. A blotch of white on the windshield established that a sizable bird had flown over, and the entire vehicle, under the layer of dirt, offered no more shine than a cinder block. Julie looked toward where her garden hose was coiled neatly under the faucet on the side of the barn. The Happy Car do-it-yourself car wash in Coldwater had closed down months ago due to the strict water restrictions.

She put the folder containing her story and her purse in the truck, ducking away from the thick heat that poured from the cab when she opened the door. She closed the door and began walking toward her hose and faucet.

How much water would it take just to hose off the dirt? What difference would it make? She thought of Ken Townsend's always-gleaming cruiser. *He must wash his car daily. Why can't a civilian have the same right?* The shiny police car was replaced in her mind with a headline:

**Selfish Woman Uses Last of Montana's Water
"My Truck Was Dirty," She Tells Rest of State**

Julie stopped halfway to the hose, sighed audibly, and turned back to her vehicle. The engine cranked a little longer than usual as she started it, but it quickly settled down to a smooth idle.

Tumbleweeds still dotted the road, and other junk—pieces of newspaper, broken sections of boards, and the occasional twisted lawn chair—made slow driving mandatory. The Coldwater radio station told Julie nothing she didn't already know, and the lilting perkiness of the announcer's voice grated on her nerves. She imagined the woman giving the news that the world was ending and making it sound as if she were speaking at a five-year-old's birthday party. The thought brought a smile to Julie's face.

The Bulldogger, she noticed, was open for business at

twenty minutes after 7:00, and a few trucks and cars rested in the shabby parking lot outside the structure. Her skid marks were still visible on the road, although traffic and the storm had scuffed away the stark blackness of the tracks.

Nancy Lewis's car was in its assigned spot at the office, as Julie knew it would be. The Celica was as dirty as her truck, which gave Julie's mood a perverse boost. She parked, gathered up her story and purse, and walked to the back door of the *News-Express*. Julie felt good in the building, just as she always did. Journalism was much more than a job and a paycheck to her, and her work at the paper seemed to become more fulfilling on a daily basis.

Most of the offices and cubicles were still dark, but the corridor lights were always on, and the air-conditioning made the sweltering temperature outside seem far away. Julie stopped and sniffed the air. Shortly after being hired, she swore that she could smell fresh newsprint and printer's ink each time she entered the building. Another reporter told her that with all the federal air filtration equipment in place, that was impossible.

"You're still a little wet behind the ears, Julie," he'd said. "One day when you're buried in memos and stories and directives and meetings, this will only be a place to work, nothing magical about it." That day hadn't yet arrived for Julie Downs, and she was quite sure that it never would.

Nancy's door was open, and she motioned Julie in.

"I have my first installment here," Julie said. "I hoped you could take a peek at it."

Nancy smiled. "You're under no obligation to hand deliver

your pieces, Julie. They'll eventually reach my desk anyway. But sure—I'll be happy to give it a look. And I'm glad you're here. I wanted to talk with you about a call—"

The phone on Nancy's desk rang, cutting off her sentence. She picked up the receiver. "Nancy Lewis," she said. She listened for a moment and then covered the mouthpiece. "Give me a few minutes, OK?"

Julie put her folder on Nancy's desk and left her boss's office, shutting the door behind her. There would be coffee—and perhaps donuts and bagels—in the break room, she knew, and she headed there.

Elisha hid something under the edge of the long table she was sitting at as Julie approached her. "Hey," she said, quickly looking away.

"Let's see it," Julie said.

"See what?"

Julie smiled. "You owe me a lunch, Leesh. A bet's a bet. Now, let me see it."

Elisha sighed dramatically. "OK, I've been cleaning dirt out of my house for the last twenty hours, and it's still like a sandbox. Mike's been driving me nuts about going riding with you. My dog rolled in something dead, and he smells like a toxic garbage pit. If you're going to hold me to a silly bet because I decided to pick up a tiny bit of comfort food today . . ." She brought her hand out from under the table; she was holding a pastry that looked to be the size of a catcher's glove. The sugar glaze twinkled in the bright light of the room, and a thumb-sized blob of fluffy white hanging from one end indicated that the treat was cream filled.

149

"Wow, I've already gained four pounds just looking at that thing."

"I've got an idea," Elisha said. "If we split this, no one's really won or lost the bet, right? The deal was whoever has a morning pastry first buys lunch—but if we share this wonderful thing, well, what's the harm?"

Julie laughed, turning to the coffeepot. "Seems fair to me."

Fifteen minutes later Julie was walking down the hall to her managing editor's office, sated with coffee and a slab of pastry she'd already begun to regret. Julie tapped on the door frame, and Nancy smiled, picking up the folder holding the story.

"Very good writing, Julie," she said. "I like the action of the language—the way you took what could have been a mere interview and balanced the whole thing with Otis's comments at the end."

"That's good to hear," Julie said. "I want the piece to work."

"Well, I hardly put a mark on it. I thought you were gushing a bit at the end of page two and on to page three, but I left most of it intact. The pictures are good too. That shot of the cornfield is frightening."

Nancy leaned back in her chair. "So, I'll run it a week from Wednesday, and we'll begin the advertising for it in tomorrow's edition." She paused for a moment. "What's next, Julie? Anything you want to talk about?"

"I have a couple of ideas, but nothing solid yet. I'm hoping for a piece focusing on cattle and horses next—some of the economics and realities of those businesses. I don't want a strictly money-oriented story, but the livestock people make up a good percentage of our population, and they're hurting as badly as the farmers."

"Maggie Lane will be a good one to talk to about the horses," Nancy said.

"Right. There's Andy Buckler who raises Appaloosas, and several others too."

"I imagine Dr. Pulver could help you out with information about how the drought and the heat affect horses and cattle."

"Right. I'll be talking to him." She smiled. "In fact, he's coming to dinner at my place on Wednesday night."

Nancy's eyebrows rose quizzically. "Mmm?"

"No further comment at this time," Julie said.

"Fair enough, then—for now." Nancy's face became more serious. "I said earlier I needed to talk with you this morning. I got a call Friday night—at home—that bothered me a bit."

"Oh?" Julie asked.

"It was from Ross Craig."

"The chief of police? What did he want?"

"Well, it was a little strange. He said he'd received a complaint from what he referred to as 'an honest businessman in the community' that you'd been to this person's business, harassing him, trying to dig up dirt for a story."

Julie groaned. "It had to be Rick Castle from the Bull-dogger. I haven't interviewed any other businesspeople, and I certainly haven't harassed anyone."

"I know that," Nancy said. "What concerns me is that there may be more of a relationship between Castle and Craig than we realize. We know that Castle is bending the rules, and I can't help but wonder what else is going on with Craig as his advocate."

"I see what you mean," Julie said. "Should I look into it?"

"No," Nancy said emphatically. "You shouldn't. I want you to leave it completely alone for now, at least." She toyed with her pen for a moment. "I made some calls to contacts yesterday," she continued. "I don't much like what I found out. Ross Craig has been quietly running a little fiefdom in Coldwater. He doesn't like being prodded by the press or anyone else, I learned. It seems to me that a man with the kind of power a police chief has could turn out to be a rather dangerous enemy, if it came to that."

"I wasn't aware of any of this," Julie said.

"Not many people are, I don't think. Or, if they are, they keep quiet about it."

"So, is there corruption here?" Julie asked. "That's a little frightening. Other than the intro piece I did on Ken Townsend, the *News-Express* hasn't given much press to the police department. They do their job, we see them around on the roads, and that's pretty much it."

"I don't know if there's corruption," Nancy said. "I heard an allegation of abuse of power from a source, but that's all it is—an allegation. For that matter, I'm not sure how good the source is."

Julie thought for a moment. "You pulled me off the Bulldogger story in no uncertain terms. I haven't been poking around at it behind your back, if that's what Craig was implying."

"I know that, Julie. I just want you to be careful, OK? Something touched a nerve in the chief, and I didn't like his telephone call."

Julie felt a quick shiver. "I'm not sure what you're saying."

Nancy's smile looked a bit artificial. "Just this—I'm going to be looking into all this very carefully through contacts in the capital and in the state police. I just wanted you to know that there may be a problem, and to be . . . well, careful, is all."

"Careful of what?"

Nancy held up her hands. "Careful of the people involved with the Coldwater PD, including the chief. I know that's cryptic, but take my word for it." Again, her smile appeared forced to Julie. "I've said too much already. Let's drop the subject for the time being, OK?"

Julie nodded at the same time her stomach rumbled loudly. She winced in pain.

Nancy stood behind her desk. "Are you all right? You look kind of pale."

Julie put both hands over her stomach. "It's all Leesha's fault," she said weakly.

Nancy laughed. "Did she stop at the bakery again? I swear, the two of you are built like broom handles, and yet you eat those hideous buns and things and never gain a pound."

"Never again," Julie said. "I feel like I've eaten an anvil."

"Can I get you some water or anything?"

"No—no thanks. I'll be fine. But I mean it—no pastries again, ever. When I even think of that monster donut we ate . . ."

"Get yourself an Alka-Seltzer. You look like you could use it. And again—fine work on the first of the series. I'll see you later."

Elisha was at her desk as Julie walked out. She was stripping the paper off a roll of Tums. As their eyes met, Elisha dropped her Tums onto her desk and made the old Valley Girl gesture—an index finger pointed directly into her wide-open mouth. Julie grimaced and nodded in agreement.

Some Coca-Cola syrup will do it, Julie thought as she started her truck. *I'll just sip at some of that soothing, cool syrup and I'll be fine. Or maybe an Alka-Seltzer like Nancy recommended.*

She pulled out of the *News-Express* parking lot and turned onto Main Street. Another reporter in his Mazda Miata honked his horn at Julie as he went into the lot, and she waved. She noted that his little sports car was as much a mess as her truck. She headed down Main Street toward her home. Averil Hildebrand was just unlocking the door to his drugstore, and Julie swung to the curb. In a matter of a few minutes she was on her way home with a package of Alka-Seltzer and two rolls of Tums.

As it almost always was, the two-lane road leading to her home was void of traffic. She eased her truck around the few curves at a cautious speed, still concerned about storm trash in the road. She was attempting to open a roll of Tums with her right hand while steering with her left when she heard the aggressive roar of a powerful engine and the bleep of a siren. She flicked her eyes to her rearview mirror and watched as the snout of a Chevrolet Blazer with a light bar flashing on its top raced up behind her.

"What in the world does he want?" she mumbled aloud. Her eyes flicked to the speedometer; she was well within the legal limit.

Julie pulled to the shoulder, shifted to neutral, and applied her parking brake. She unfastened her safety belt and began to open her door when a tinny, overly loud amplified voice warned her, "Driver, do not exit your vehicle. Turn off your engine and placc both hands at the top of your steering wheel and wait until I approach you."

Still confused, Julie complied. She watched in her rearview as Ross Craig, in full uniform including hat, stopped twenty or so feet behind her on the shoulder with the light bar atop his cruiser still operating. He exited his car and began walking toward her.

The chief was six feet or slightly taller, with a barrel-like, stocky body. He was in his early fifties, and a good deal of gray was visible in his buzz-cut brownish hair.

"Driver—keep both your hands at the top of the steering wheel," Ross Craig said as he approached Julie's truck.

For a moment Julie felt the urge to snap the clutch and leave this man behind. That, she realized, would be foolish. She turned her key to the off position. She lost Craig's reflection in her mirror as he bent down at the rear of her truck.

Julie felt her truck shift the very slightest bit on its frame, and then she heard a tapping sound. It came again—the tapping sound, but this time a bit harder—and was followed by the tinkling of smashed glass. The officer was again in her mirror, and then he was at her door.

"Ma'am, you're driving with a non-operative taillight," Craig said as he peered in her window. "That's in violation of the State of Montana Road and Vehicle Statutes, and I could write you a summons. Please hand me your driver's license, insurance information, and the registration to this vehicle."

Julie focused on her dashboard for a moment, swallowed, and said, "There was nothing wrong with my taillight until you broke it. I don't know what you're trying to pull here . . ."

Craig leaned down to look into the window, his face a few inches from Julie's.

"Driver," he said, "I'll need your operator's license, registration, and proof of insurance. Please hand it to me."

Julie grabbed her purse from the floor in front of the passenger's seat. The purse was full of scraps of paper with scrawled notes and telephone numbers of story sources, some loose and lint-encrusted Life Savers, a lipstick case, her cell phone, a lump of Kleenex, and her wallet, which contained her license and insurance card. She located the wallet with fingers that trembled a bit, and removed the documents. The truck registration was in her glove compartment; she opened it and took out the form and handed all three to Craig.

The chief glanced at them cursorily and handed them back. "You know," he said in an almost conversational tone, "bothering honest businessmen can get a person in trouble in my town."

"Look, Mr. Craig—"

"It's Chief Craig," the man said, his tone now harder. "And you look, Ms. Downs—I don't allow harassment of my constituents by scribblers from throwaway newspapers. Are we clear on that?"

Julie took a breath and held it for a moment before speaking. "I'm afraid I don't know what you're talking about," she said.

There was no mistaking the steel in Craig's voice now. "You know exactly what I'm talking about. If I see one word about the Bulldogger in your scandal sheet or hear that you've pestered Castle again, you'll have a lot more trouble than you can handle."

Julie bit back a response. She broke eye contact with Craig and stared straight ahead through her windshield. She heard the chief's boots move on the gravel of the road as he began to turn away from her truck. "No ticket this time—just a warning. Get that bad taillight fixed," he growled over his shoulder.

Julie watched in her rearview, hands white-knuckled on her steering wheel, as Craig climbed into his Blazer. The roof lights went out, and the engine started, and the SUV swept past her truck. Then, he was gone from her vision after he rounded a curve. Julie sat very still, not moving to turn the key, to drive away.

157

Should I call Nancy and tell her about this? Should I get in touch with the state police? She took several deep breaths and exhaled slowly, evenly, unclenching her death grip on the steering wheel. *It's my word against that of the chief of police. My taillight is broken—even though he broke it. There's no record of the conversation, of his threats, of his attempt to intimidate me.*

The yoga-style breathing helped a great deal. Within a couple of minutes the quiver was gone from Julie's hands and her thoughts were no longer racing. *I'll keep this to myself for now. I'm off the story, and I have no reason to see Castle again. Nancy's working on something to do with Craig. I'll leave him to her.*

Julie tugged her shoulder harness into place and started her engine. She noticed the partially unwrapped roll of Tums on the passenger seat. At least the stress of the encounter had forced her to forget about her upset stomach. She eased away from the side of the road and headed for home. She'd made a decision—at least a decision of sorts. Why then, she wondered, did she feel so uneasy?

Danny was on an extension ladder leaning against the top of the big sliding front door of her barn when Julie rolled up her driveway. He was near the top of the ladder, swiping at the track upon which the wooden door rode, with a section torn from a burlap grain sack in one hand and an old-fashioned spouted oil can in the other. Sunday stood nervously at the bottom of the ladder, peering upward.

The first thing Julie heard when she got out of her truck after parking it next to Danny's truck was a high-pitched, intermittent whining sound that varied in tone, almost as if the frightened dog was attempting to communicate some bizarre canine language.

"Almost done, Julie," Danny called down without looking too far away from his work. "The track was really packed—it's no wonder we could hardly open the door Saturday."

Sunday raced to Julie, whined for a second, and then ran back to his post at the base of the ladder.

"Looks like somebody doesn't like to see you way up there," Julie said. "This poor ol' dog is gonna jump out of his skin." After a moment, she added, "It isn't my favorite thing either. This ladder looks a bit . . . rickety, doesn't it?"

"It's a little beat up," Danny answered, "but it's a good, sturdy ladder. Made out of maple." Then he mumbled, "Or something. Anyway, I'm almost done."

Sunday increased his whining on hearing Danny speak. Together, the dog and Julie watched as Danny finished up the job, dropped the piece of burlap, and began downward, holding the oil can in one hand. Sunday's carrying on stopped the moment the man was on solid ground.

"It'll be smooth as can be now," Danny said proudly. "And look—your kitchen window is in. All you gotta do is paint the frame and replace that length of siding."

"Wow! Thanks a ton, Danny. You're a regular Mr. Fix-it. You charged the window to me, right?"

Danny nodded. "Got a good deal on it too. Whew—it's hotter'n blue blazes up there."

159

"C'mon—let's go inside. Get out of the sun. I've got a big pitcher of iced tea all set to go."

They walked to the kitchen door side by side, Sunday trailing behind. "Business slow today?" Julie asked as she opened the door. "Hey!" she exclaimed. "You put a new thingie in the door!"

Danny laughed. "Those thingies are called linchpins, and yep, I replaced them and tightened up the plates. Just another service of Mr. Fix-it, jack-of-all-trades—"

"And master of none," they finished together.

Danny sat at the kitchen table while Julie poured iced tea. "Yeah, it's slow today," he answered her earlier question. "No clinic appointments and no field calls either. I've got my cell with me in case of emergencies, but no calls so far." He took a long drink of iced tea. "What about you? All done for the day before noon? I figured I'd be long gone by the time you got home."

"I'm glad I caught you then—a man needs a cold drink after fixing barns and houses. I don't have much going on right now either. I dropped my first piece in my series at the office."

"What was the reaction from your boss to this one?"

"Nancy liked it." Julie beamed. "It'll run a week from Wednesday, and the advertising for it will start tomorrow."

"That's great, Julie." Danny drank again. "So here we are, both working banker's hours with nothing much to do."

"Mmm. Feels kind of good," Julie agreed. "If one of us had a swimming pool . . ."

Danny smiled at her, and she could see his mind working.

"What?" she asked.

"I have an idea. I was at the Tozek ranch last week. Myron and I had to use his ATV to get to a pond way back on his land, past that south pasture of his. It's a couple of miles, and the ground is too rough even for a truck. He had a colicky cow that he didn't want to move. I didn't even know there was a pond back there—but you ought to see it, Julie. It's spring fed and crystal clear. Myron says it's quite a bit lower this year than it has been in the past, but it's still maybe five feet or so deep in the middle. He said there are people there daily—teens and adults. There was a bunch of Boy Scouts there the day I was."

"Sounds nice," Julie said. "Most of the ponds I've heard about are either mud puddles now or completely gone."

"Myron offered me the use of the pond for a swim. Since we're not doing anything, how about it? Feel like cooling off?"

"Walking out there in this heat?"

"Why walk? We hook up your trailer, load Drifter, go to my place and pick up Dakota, and off we go."

Julie hesitated, and then a smile took over her face. "Let's do it!"

"The water's so cold it'll crack your teeth. Imagine how it'd feel on a day like today. Plus, our horses have been getting very little use. It'll be good for them too. Heck—we don't even have to saddle them. It's only a couple of miles. We can ride bareback."

"Yeah," Julie said. "Sounds great." She grinned at Danny. "You said the water's cold?"

161

"We'll have to dig through a foot of ice to even get to the water."

"A foot?"

"Absolutely. At least a foot."

Julie was on her feet and dashing to the stairway. "Then let's get in gear," she called over her shoulder. "I'll get into my bathing suit and grab a couple of towels."

By the time Julie came out of the kitchen door, Danny had backed her truck around to the front of her two-horse trailer and was plugging in the brake-light connection. Julie checked the union of the trailer and the ball installed on her rear bumper and made certain the safety chain was properly attached. Then she fetched Drifter from his usual place under the trees in the pasture. Fortunately, he hadn't rolled today, and his back and withers were clean.

The heat in the open pasture was an aggressive and tenacious beast. Silky sheets of it shimmered from the arid ground in front of her and bore down on her Stetson with a palpable weight. For a brief moment she reconsidered the entire adventure—but then the thoughts of actually being cool—perhaps even cold—were so enchanting, so beguiling, that she quickened her pace leading Drifter back to the barn.

The horse loaded easily and calmly, as he'd been trained to do. He walked up the ramp at the rear of the trailer with no silliness and moved to his position on the right side of the central divider. Julie snapped his halter to a short lead line, attached the butt-strap behind him, and closed and latched the back door. She moved to the driver's side of the truck, climbed in, and smiled at Danny. Then, they were off.

Sunday wasn't pleased when Danny ordered him into the mudroom at his home, but as ever he obeyed, if a bit reluctantly. The two-mile trek would be too much for a collie carrying a full coat. Dakota, Danny's Appaloosa gelding, loaded as readily as Drifter had. The two horses snuffed at one another from opposite sides of the divider, but they'd been used together before, and there was no squabbling between them.

As Julie drove, Danny called Myron Tozek and told the rancher he was taking him up on his kind offer, and that he and Julie were going to ride their horses to the pond. When he'd disconnected, he said to Julie, "Myron says to leave the trailer at his second gate and just go cross-country over what should have been his wheat crop. He said there's nothing there we can hurt."

Julie nodded. She knew where the gate was—and also knew that rather than allowing passage to Myron's combines and tractors to his nine-hundred-plus acres of wheat, the fence and the gate did nothing but keep tumbleweeds confined. She pulled well off the road, and they unloaded their horses. Danny opened the gate, and when they'd passed through it, he secured it again. Farm manners were farm manners—drought or no drought.

They gathered their reins and swung aboard their horses, riding bareback, as they'd decided. The horses worked well, seemingly revitalized by the change of scenery, shedding their heat-generated lethargy. Julie and Danny settled their mounts into a comfortable jog and rode straight across the huge and barren section of land. Julie looked behind them once and was reminded of the western movies she'd loved as a youngster. A thick, narrow cloud of dust hung in the air, raised by the horses' hooves.

"It's a good thing we didn't rob a bank," she told Danny, motioning him to look back. "The good guys would find us in a second."

The pond was perfect—a jewel in a desert, pretty enough to be a mirage. It was small—maybe a quarter of an acre—and loosely surrounded by willows. A few cattle stood in the water, drinking. A few others eyed the horses and riders suspiciously. The Scouts were back, throwing a ball at one another at one end of the pond in a game that apparently involved a great deal of yelling, laughing, and dunking.

"Myron didn't see any reason not to let the cattle wander over here to drink," Danny explained. "But there's no pasture for them. They drink and then head back. That's how the cow I treated came to be out here."

"I don't know if it's because it's so stunning in itself or because I haven't seen anything like it in a long time—but it's gorgeous. Let's tie these guys and hit the water!"

For the tiniest part of a second Julie was disappointed as she cleaved the pond's surface. Then, when she'd penetrated the foot or so of sun-heated water and moved her body deeper, she was struck by an almost electrical shock of delightfully arctic springwater. The cold poured over her, and the physical transformation from the ninety-plus degrees and brazen sun to the pristine clarity and gripping frigidity of the pond's bottom was purely delicious.

Danny, a yard or so to Julie's side, flashed her a thumbs-up hand signal. She returned it. They surfaced together, sucking air, invigorated and laughing from the joy of the experience. They swam toward the Scouts' game, and a couple of the boys recognized Danny. "Doc Pulver—wanna play bombardment?"

"Maybe in a bit," Danny called. "Thanks for the invite."

After savoring the chilliness, Julie noticed that a strange and long absent physical phenomena had taken place: she was shivering. She turned to shore and swam gracefully, gliding through the upper layer of warmer water. Danny joined her, and together they waded to shore and sat on the towels Julie had brought, letting the sun dry them.

"Those boys must be immune to cold," Julie said, motioning toward the Scouts.

"The water's shallow there where they're playing—warmer," Danny pointed out. "Even so, I can remember playing water polo when I was eleven or twelve and having my lips turn blue from the cold. Kids don't worry about stuff like that."

For the first time in a long time, the sun seemed benign as it dried them.

"I'm glad we did this, Danny," Julie said. "I think I needed it, or something like it. A break, I guess. It's good to escape for a couple of hours."

"Yeah," Danny agreed. "I'm glad I could do this—not only to cool off but to spend some time with a good friend. It kinda recharges the batteries. I wish we could have brought Sunny, though. He'd love this."

Friends?

Julie avoided the "friends" comment, not at all sure how Danny had meant it. "Maybe when things cool down, we can bring him out. Does he like the water?"

Danny laughed. "He loves it. Wait until you see him after he's been chasing sticks and is completely soaked. That big dog looks like a drowned rat when his coat is sticking to his frame."

"Yo—Doc Pulver! Come on, we need another player!" One of the Scouts waved at Danny.

"Umm . . . would you mind?" Danny asked.

Julie flashed on an image of a young boy asking for a cookie. She smiled at Danny. "Go get 'em," she laughed. "I'm happy just to sit here and feel good." She pretended to sulk. "Anyway, they didn't invite me."

"Give them a few years, and they'll invite you and ignore me," Danny said.

"Go play with your little friends," she said with a laugh. She settled back on her elbows and watched Danny lope over to the group of boys. *It's funny how men never really grow up,* she thought. *How they remain kids—boys—in so many ways.* The game of bombardment was a simple one—whack the other players with the ball before they had time to duck under water. Danny was being hit far more often than he was hitting the others, and Julie noticed that many of his throws were wildly off target. When Danny did strike a boy with the ball, the throw was invariably an easy toss. That simple kindness touched Julie's heart to the point where she had to swallow hard a couple of times to remove the lump in her throat.

Intrinsic kindness—how rare that seems to be, and how much of it Danny has. His comment about good friends came to mind. *Is that how he sees me? As a friend rather than as something more in his life? But then why did he kiss me the other day?* The lazy, uncomplicated pleasure of the afternoon seemed to recede from Julie like an ocean tide. *How much time does a guy need to realize that a woman is interested in him—interested beyond friendship?*

She stood and walked to where they'd left the horses. Drifter was half asleep, standing in the speckled shade provided by a willow tree, and Dakota, tied a few yards away, looked as bored as a horse could possibly be.

Julie shook her head, attempting to chase away the irritability that had so suddenly taken over. Shouts and laughter from the boys—and from Danny—reached her.

This is absolutely and unremittingly silly, she scolded herself. *It's a fine afternoon. Why wreck it? What's going to happen will happen. What else can I do? Send him a Candy-Gram? Sing under his window?* Again, a headline stood boldly and clearly in her mind:

Surly Woman Sulks, Destroys Good Time

When she returned to the towels, Danny was on his, leaning back on his elbows, eyes closed, letting the sun dry him.

167

"Kids wear you out?" she asked, sitting on her towel.

Danny smiled, his eyes still closed against the sun. "Those kids know what fun is. They'd rather be right there playing their game than anywhere else in the world." He reflected for a minute. "I'm enjoying myself more today than I have in a long time. I . . : I'm glad you're here."

"I'm glad I'm here too, Danny," Julie said softly. *Now, if he'd take my hand . . .*

He didn't. Instead he looked over at the Scouts, who'd finally left the water and were packing their gear into backpacks. "I guess we ought to get back too," Danny said. "I've got a desk covered with papers I need to push around."

"And I've got some calls to make. Oh—also—I'd like to interview you Wednesday at dinner for my next drought piece. I'm going to focus on what's happening in the cattle and horse industries."

"Sure," Danny agreed quickly. "I just got a batch of statistics from the state that might be something you'd like to look at. Peripheral stuff, in a sense—but not so peripheral when you think about it. Feed grain harvests, hay—all that."

"That'd probably save me some Internet research time. Thanks. But we'll probably bore poor Ken to death with our shop talk."

"I doubt that very much," Danny said.

Julie met his eyes. "What do you mean?"

"I think the guy's interested in you, Julie."

She felt her heart beat faster. "What makes you say that?"

"Well . . . the way he looked at you several times Saturday

168

night—stuff like that. He wanted to know how long we'd ..." He hesitated. "He wanted to know things about you. Nothing really intrusive and nothing personal, but it seemed like more than normal curiosity. That's all."

Julie scrambled for a response. The best she could do was, "He could be just looking for a friend."

"Maybe so," Danny said quickly, standing. "Look—it's a long, hot ride back to the trailer. If we don't take advantage of the pond once more, we'll wish we had."

Julie thought it over. She was dry, but she was already sweltering. Danny was right—it was a long and dusty ride to her truck.

"You talked me into it," she said, laughing. She got to her feet. "Last one in is a hog's uncle!" she yelled as she ran toward the water's edge.

At the trailer and after the horses were loaded, Danny offered to drive. Julie accepted. It wasn't a long distance, but she was sleepy from the short night before and from the swimming. She rested against the passenger door and closed her eyes. She and Danny rode in companionable silence, the air-conditioning fighting off the late afternoon heat.

Julie hadn't given much thought to Danny's comment about Ken Townsend—and as she semi-dozed, she didn't care to wrestle with it. The episode with Chief Craig earlier in the day returned to her but without the stress of the confrontation. The hours passing had, in a sense, diminished the event. *Big-frog-in-a-small-pond syndrome?* she wondered. *A cop perhaps too protective of his drinking buddy?* Or was there more to the whole thing? Had showing up at the Bulldogger to interview Castle—and her fabrication about the videotape—upset something she knew nothing about? *Nah. If there's anything there, Nancy will find it. I ought to send a bill for my taillight lens to that jerk, though.*

Danny lowering the back gate of the trailer awakened Julie. Her eyes felt gritty, and she noticed now that her nose and cheeks were tingling with a light sunburn. She shook off her grogginess and joined Danny as he led Dakota back to his pasture.

"Hey, sleepyhead," he greeted her.

"Too much sun, I guess. Felt good to nap for a few minutes, though."

"Should I put on some coffee? Or would you like iced tea or a soda?"

"No—no thanks. Let's get to my place so I can unload Drifter and you can get your truck. Then I think I'll try to continue right along with the nap I started."

Danny drove to Julie's farm and backed the trailer into its spot next to the barn. Julie dropped the gate and let Drifter back out on his own. She led him into the fresh stall she'd prepared that morning. Then she walked with Danny to his truck.

"Thanks for the horse-hauling and the fun afternoon," Danny said. "We'll have to do it again sometime."

"I should be thanking you—for all the work you've done around here. And sure, I'd love to do it again. Maybe next

170

time we could bring sandwiches and drinks and paperback books and make a day of it."

Danny opened the driver's door of his truck and then turned back to Julie. A moment passed that made Julie feel self-conscious, and she wondered if Danny was experiencing the same thing. His right hand began to rise but stopped and returned to his side. He climbed behind the steering wheel. "That'd be fun. I'll see you Wednesday about 7:00, then?"

"Bring your appetite. I'm gonna feed you guys until you fall over."

"I'm looking forward to it." Danny started his engine, waved to Julie, and started down the driveway. Julie watched until he turned onto the road, and then went into her house.

It was only a couple of degrees cooler in the kitchen, but it felt good to be home. Her fatigue seemed to have drifted off, and a nap no longer seemed enticing. She sat at the kitchen table with a legal pad and a ballpoint, deciding what she needed for the feast Wednesday evening. *The steaks are easy enough: two twenty-two ouncers and one twelve-ounce. A big soup bone for Sunny. Garlic bread. Romaine lettuce, olives, cukes, Spanish onion, croutons, tomatoes for the salad. Potatoes for baking. Should I make a dessert? Nah—Ben and Jerry'll take care of that . . .*

She shoved the list across the table, knowing that even if she completed it, the page would most likely remain in her purse as she did her customarily "grab, run, and overspend" type of shopping. She sat back in her chair, very aware that a sort of uneasiness had enveloped her—a light nervousness that made her feel as if she'd left something important undone. When the telephone rang, Julie started as if a bomb had gone off. She pushed her chair back and walked to the phone, letting it ring twice more before she picked it up.

"Julie Downs."

"Julie, it's Maggie. Ian's at the church until late tonight with the youth ministry, and I'm soooo lonely." She sighed dramatically. "If only a friend would ask me over for a cup of coffee. But I guess that's too much to hope for . . ."

"Ya goof." Julie laughed. "C'mon over. I'm just sitting around leaping out of my skin."

"Oh? Why? What's the problem?"

"No problem, I guess. I'm just a little nervous and jerky, is all. I'll probably talk your ear off. See you in a few, OK? I'll put coffee on."

"Just the thing when you're a little edgy is that super-strong coffee you make," Maggie noted sarcastically. "How about tea?"

"Good point. I'll put the kettle on."

Julie hung up the receiver and smiled to herself. *That's what best friends are for.*

In the twenty or so minutes until her guest arrived, Julie took herself to task. She realized and finally admitted to herself that she did know what was bothering her—and it had nothing to do with Ross Craig or a story for the *News-Express*. It was the afternoon she'd spent with Danny and the simple fact that throughout the afternoon his words had confused her. Almost equally disconcerting, she had to admit, were the frequent thoughts of Ken Townsend that came to her unbidden.

She moved about the kitchen, mumbling to herself at times, wondering how she was going to articulate all this to Maggie. Julie was rubbing aloe on her cheeks and nose in the bathroom when her friend pulled into the driveway. She hurried down the stairs as Maggie came in through the kitchen door. They smiled at one another.

"Sunburn? Out riding in this heat?" Maggie asked.

"Sit," Julie instructed, turning the flame on under the pot and taking teacups from the cupboard. "And then listen, OK?"

Maggie nodded.

Julie related the events of the afternoon, including direct quotes from Danny as well as his feeling that Ken was "interested" in her, and ended with how Danny's hand had begun to move to her as she stood at the open door of his truck and then halted so abruptly.

Maggie sipped her tea for a few moments after Julie finished speaking. "What's going on with you and Ken?" she asked. "Is there something there?"

"No," Julie answered too quickly. Then she admitted, "I don't know."

"Mmm," Maggie breathed noncommittally. "It doesn't seem like Danny is responding to you, does it? Or at least not in the way you'd like him to."

Julie nodded. "Right. And before you ask—I'm not pushing the guy. I'm really not. I think he cares about me, but there's something that stops him from doing anything about it. I can't figure it out."

"You know," Maggie said quietly, her eyes meeting Julie's, "there's a possibility that Danny simply isn't ready for a romantic relationship. I'm sorry, Julie. But there's that possibility."

Julie looked down at her now empty teacup. "Yeah," she breathed.

Maggie got up from her chair and walked to the stove, where she turned on the burner under the pot. "I saw a lot of Danny before I married Ian. And Danny was pretty serious about me."

The kettle began to hiss.

"Is he over you, do you think? Really over you?"

"Yes," Maggie said emphatically. "We talked about it a year or so ago. I'm convinced that he's not carrying a torch for me." Maggie added boiling water to both their cups. "I wish I knew what to tell you other than that."

Julie sighed. "So do I."

8

Julie poked at the charcoal in her portable grill set up outside her kitchen. The embers were a nicely uniform gray-white over a bed of glowing red. "If Danny Pulver is one thing, it's punctual," she said to Ken.

Ken, looking quite comfortable in one of the three folding lawn chairs Julie had picked up the day before in her shopping expedition, took a long drink from his tall glass of iced tea. "I came across a couple of my old car magazines that featured the Ford 427 Interceptor. I brought them along for him—he's interested in the muscle cars, the dragsters, all that stuff."

Julie turned from the grill. "I didn't know that about him until he mentioned it at Drago's the night of the storm. Seems strange—a veterinary doctor who's a . . . what was that term? A gearbox?"

"Gearhead." Ken laughed. "He knows what he's talking about too. He had a hot Chev when he was in high school. Just like me, he put every penny he could scrounge up into that car. I was a Chrysler man at the time, but those Chevs were something."

"Did you race?" Julie asked.

"Sure." Ken grinned. "Quarter-mile drags—not NAS-CAR-type racing."

"Isn't that kind of dangerous for a high school kid?"

"There's not much danger in drags—'cept the danger of blowing up a four- or five-thousand-dollar engine with several hundred hours of sweat and labor put into it."

"I've seen some of it on TV," Julie said. "Looks like fun."

"It is. I once figured out," he mused, "that each little trophy I won with my Hemi cost me about a hundred and fifty dollars in building my engine—and that's not including anything for my labor."

"Not really cost effective?"

"Not at all. But a heck of a lot of fun."

Julie looked at her watch and then back at the fire. "It's twenty after 7:00. Since Danny hasn't called, I'm sure he's just running a little late. I don't want to lose the peak of the fire, so I'm going to put the steaks on."

"Anything I can do for you?"

"Eat some more chips and dip and drink some more iced tea, is all. Everything's under control."

When Julie came back out carrying a large platter with the meat on it, Ken gaped and then laughed. "Wow! That's the better part of a cow, isn't it?"

"I didn't think either of you guys was a light eater—and these aren't the better part of a cow. They're the best. At least the best steaks Louie's Meat Market had to offer, and he has wonderful beef."

"You really didn't have to do all this, Julie. Don't get me wrong—I'm glad you did. But can't I at least help out with a couple bucks toward the meat?"

"Absolutely not! You didn't have to help with the cleanup, but you did. Fair's fair, Ken." She checked her watch again, a bit concerned this time, and looked at the fire. The coals were the slightest bit beyond prime for broiling, showing more gray ash than a few minutes ago but still very hot.

Julie made her decision. She set the platter on the table and with a long barbecue fork arranged the two massive steaks and the third smaller one on the surface of the grill, where they hissed cheerfully, sending up a cloud of blue smoke as fat hit the embers.

"No choice, Ken—this is the last of my charcoal, and the fire's backing down. Danny'll be here in a minute."

Julie's cell phone buzzed in her pocket. "Julie Downs," she said, hoping that Danny wasn't on the other end of the connection.

"Julie," Danny said, "this is the first second I've had to call in a couple of hours. Roger Hart's Clydesdale mare is giving birth and having a very tough time of it." Danny rarely sounded rushed or harried, but he did now. "I'm sorry about dinner—you and Ken go ahead, if you haven't already. From the looks of things, I'm going to be here for a long time. She's—"

Julie heard a horse squeal in the background and a male voice shout, "Doc!"

"Gotta go, Julie. Sorry." And then Danny was gone.

Julie folded her telephone and returned it to her pocket.

177

"Well," she said glumly to Ken, "three guesses as to who that was."

"Danny have an emergency?"

"Yeah. A Clydesdale is foaling, and Danny says she's in trouble. He can't get away—couldn't even talk for a minute. He wants us to go ahead without him."

Ken looked over at the flaming steaks. "We don't have much choice, do we? Not unless we want to waste an awful lot of good beef. Can you take one of the big ones off and keep it for Danny?"

Julie shook her head. "They're almost half-cooked now. Have you ever tasted a steak that was reheated after being broiled? It's like trying to eat a saddle. I guess Sunday will enjoy it, though. Collies aren't picky when it comes to meat."

Ken moved from his chair to stand next to Julie. "I guess that comes with what Danny does, just like a doctor for humans. The patients don't much care about special dinners when they need help."

Julie forced a smile that became more real when she met Ken's eyes. "Well, all we can do is carry on, I guess. And how bad can a good meal and good company be?"

"My thoughts exactly. We'll include Danny next time."

The meal was splendid. The beef—cooked rare—was tender, with the rich flavor of corn-fed meat. Julie's salad was a major success—Ken refilled his bowl twice. The baked potatoes—the feast's only concession to technology since they were heated in Julie's microwave—were perfect. Julie heated the wrapped garlic bread on the edge of the grill, and when she peeled away the foil the heady aroma of toast and garlic was almost more appetizing than the scent of the steaks.

"Coffee?" Julie asked.

"Let me do it," Ken insisted. "As soon as I can move."

"Everything was good, wasn't it? I'm stuffed," Julie agreed. "If you want to get the coffee, you have my blessing. I never want to get out of this chair."

They'd eaten at a small picnic table on the shaded side of Julie's house, and now the table was covered with scraps of food, potato skins, and small crusts of garlic bread.

"Not only that, but I'll get rid of the trash," Ken said, gathering the mess onto the platter that Julie had carried the meat on. "Back in a minute. I know where the coffee is from Saturday night. If I recall, you take it black, correct?"

"Yes, black—and strong too."

When Ken came back with two steaming mugs of coffee he handed one to Julie and then arranged his lawn chair so that he was facing her. He settled himself in and sipped at his coffee. So did Julie. They were silent for several moments, enjoying the heartiness of the drink after the huge meal.

"Ahh . . . how about them Mets?" Ken said.

Julie grinned. "Are you trying to point out that even after feeding you, I need to make conversation to keep you from being bored?"

"Exactly."

"Well, then—any man's favorite subject is himself. Tell me about how your job is going and how you like Coldwater."

Ken gazed at Julie over the top of his coffee. "I like Coldwater fine, at least at this time in my life. I like the pace—the way people live and do things. It's a whole lot different than what I knew in Billings."

"You've come to us at kind of a rough time, though."

"Yeah. The drought's hard on the town and the farmers and ranchers." He hesitated for a moment before going on. "But, as your article said, these are strong people. Gutsy people who're survivors. I've come to believe that more and more strongly with each of the folks I meet. You know, when I was reading your article, I felt like I was sitting there on the porch talking with Mr. Harker."

Julie smiled. "Huller. His name is Cyrus Huller."

Ken shook his head. To Julie's amazement, he was blushing.

"Easy name to forget," Julie said with a wave of her hand. "I'm happy that you remember the gist of the piece and that it conveyed what I intended it to. What about the job? Is that working out well?"

"I think it is—in general. And the work is different. As a PI I could focus pretty much on one or two cases I was working, give them all my time. Here I have the existing cases I inherited plus my patrols plus whatever arises, from motor-vehicle accidents to wandering cattle to barroom fights to finding lost kids." He considered for a moment and then went on. "Actually, I like the police work better."

"Oh? Why?"

180

"Well, I feel like I'm accomplishing something positive here, pretty much on a daily basis. There were good things about my PI work, like bringing a runaway teen home to his or her parents or catching someone defrauding an insurance company. But as a police officer I have more human—more personal—contact with people, to be genuinely helping them."

"I don't think Magnum P.I. would agree with you, Ken."

He laughed. "I'll tell you what: send me to Hawaii and give me a Ferrari to drive, and I'll try private investigating again."

"You said 'in general' about your work, though. What do you mean by that?"

Ken hesitated for a moment.

"I'm sorry," Julie said quickly. "I don't mean to be nosy."

"No—no, it's a valid question. I'm having sort of a personality conflict with a guy I work with. I'm pretty sure—in fact, I know—it's not going to go away. We're . . . well . . . different. Widely separated in our approach to law enforcement, I guess it's fair to say." After a half minute passed, Ken said, "Plus, I think the guy is a grade-A maggot."

Before Julie could stop herself, the words left her. "Ross Craig?"

Ken was surprised, if his eyes and his body language were any indication. After a moment, he nodded solemnly. "It's not a good topic right now."

Julie stood up from her chair. "I'll refill our cups. Anything you want from inside?"

Ken held out his mug. "When you get back, you have to tell me about your life and your work."

"That won't take more than thirty seconds."

"Somehow, I can't believe that, Julie."

In half an hour, Ken made another trip to the kitchen. An hour after that, Julie went in and brought out large bowls of Cherry Garcia.

Julie was surprised when she glanced at her watch and realized that she couldn't see its face. The sun had set, but the conversation flowed on easily, interspersed with laughter. They discovered similarities between themselves, and, equally important, differences. Julie expressed her love of writing and admitted that she dreamed of one day crafting a novel; Ken told her he wanted to retire from police work at fifty and open a bookstore.

Ken checked his own watch after seeing Julie peering at hers. "Almost 11:00," he said. "I had no idea it was so late. You must be tired."

"A bit. It doesn't seem like we've been out here that long." She stood.

"Wait—hold on. Sit back down for a minute."

"Well . . . OK. What's going on?"

Ken stood in front of his chair but didn't move any closer to Julie. He cleared his throat needlessly. "I've enjoyed tonight a lot. A whole lot. I'd like to do this type of thing again—with you, I mean. I like being with you. You're easy to talk to, and you listen." He waited for a moment and then went on, his words more rapid but not to the point of tripping over one another. "The problem is that I don't know what your relationship with Danny is. I don't know how close you are, how much time you spend together, whether there's a commitment. And if you and Danny are serious about one another, I won't make a fool out of myself and lose a couple of people I'd like to have as friends."

Julie took a long time to respond. When she did, she spoke slowly, as if feeling her way into what she wanted to say. "I have feelings for Danny. But I'm not certain I'm in love with him. And I'm not sure, either, how Danny feels about me. He's a hard man to understand at times, and he doesn't show affection easily." She took a breath. "We're not . . . well . . . committed or anything, if that's what you mean. I wish I could give you a better answer, Ken. You deserve a better answer."

She took another breath. "I've had a good time tonight too. You're easy to talk to, and you make me laugh. I've enjoyed being with you." She stopped there.

"Am I hearing a 'but' coming on, Julie?" Ken asked.

Again, it was a moment before she answered. "No," she said quite distinctly, although for some reason the words wanted to stick in her throat. "No, you're not. It'd be fun to see you again. I'd like that."

She could hear the smile, the relief, in Ken's voice. "That's great," he said. "I'd better get going now. Before I mess up whatever this is."

"Good idea," Julie said. There was a smile in her voice too.

Julie fumbled with her ringing cell phone. "Julie Downs."

"Hi, Julie. Remember me?"

"Um, no, I don't," Julie said with a laugh. "Refresh my memory."

"I was at your house for dinner a couple nights ago. We had steaks and sat outside talking for several hours."

"Wait, you're the short guy, right? The accountant?"

"Close, but not quite," he said with a chuckle. "I'm tall and I'm a police officer—Officer Townsend."

"Oh, yes, that's right—of course I remember you, Curt."

He laughed again. "Close enough. The reason why I'm calling is because the Rialto is running *Young Frankenstein* and *Blazing Saddles* back-to-back Saturday night—kind of a Mel Brooks retrospective. I was wondering if you'd like to—"

"I love Mel Brooks films! What time?"

"How about I pick you up at 7:00?"

"Great. See you then, Carl."

Julie's piece on the impact of the drought on the cattle and horse industries in Coldwater was a big success. So were the topics she pursued through the next couple of months—youth and the drought, the effect on wildlife, phony rainmakers and charlatan shamans, and the perspectives of the federal government, among others. Circulation from news boxes and store sales increased appreciably each time her articles appeared, and there was a boost in home subscriptions after the *News-Express* ran her third piece. Advertising revenues were up slightly, and one of Julie's stories was nominated for a prestigious yearly award by the Montana Journalism Society.

The drought continued as autumn began to nudge at the sky-high temperatures that Montanans thought would never end. More and more business owners boarded up their stores in Coldwater and the surrounding area. Hay and feed prices skyrocketed, and ranchers began selling off cattle they could no longer afford to feed. The General Motors dealership in Coldwater closed its doors for the final time, after months of listless and then nonexistent sales. The movie theater where Julie and Ken had laughed their way through the Brooks films failed after over forty years of bringing westerns, comedies, and action-adventure to young people and family groups in Coldwater. Even Drago's—a fixture in the town—was scrambling to stay in business. It seemed as though the Bulldogger was the only entrepreneurial effort making money in Coldwater.

Julie's life was full—or at least extremely busy. Her work was going well. Story ideas from readers flooded her email daily at the *News-Express*, and many of the ideas were strong and viable. Drifter was carrying more weight than Julie liked to see on him, but she was a believer in the horseman's saying "Summer fat is worth a winter blanket." Using the horse more was simply impossible in the endless heat.

Though she wasn't able to exercise her horse as much as she liked, she was spending a lot of her free time these days with Ken Townsend. Her feelings for him—a guy who couldn't possibly treat her better in any way—had grown, she realized. But at the same time she knew that Danny was still very much on her mind and in her heart. They still spent time together, and they always had a good time. She was drawn to him, yet he made no attempt to move closer to her, to become a larger part of her life.

Is there something about me that makes Danny hesitant to commit? If so, why won't he talk about it?

Danny exhibited no jealousy whatsoever concerning her time with Ken Townsend. And, although Ken said that he realized she'd eventually have to make a choice, he was in no particular hurry. Nevertheless, Julie noticed that the few times she'd mentioned Danny to Ken, there was quick mote of concern visible in his eyes.

Danny's invitation to return to the Tozek pond for another afternoon of swimming was a welcome one. Julie had things to do and calls to make, but she gladly put them aside. The temperature was again in the mid-nineties, and the thought of the chilled water and some time spent doing nothing but talking and resting was hugely appealing. She put a piece of good cheddar, a half loaf of Italian bread, a plastic milk container she'd filled with water and frozen, and four bottles of cold springwater in a drawstring bag and was ready to go.

This time, Julie picked up Danny and his Appaloosa with Drifter already loaded in her trailer. Dakota, she noticed, had gained some weight he didn't really need.

"I know," Danny said when she commented on it. "I cut back on the sweet feed, but that's not the problem. He needs exercise, but with things the way they've been, putting miles on him would probably do more harm than good. Probably to both of us," he added. "I was inoculating Sam McKee's ewes the other day out in his smaller pasture. I found myself facedown in the dirt—didn't even know what hit me. I just kind of fainted. I suppose it was my fault since I'd left my hat in my truck. It scared me, though—and reminded me that this kind of weather is nothing to play around with."

"I talked with Sarah Morrison yesterday," Julie said. "She told me that the ER at Coldwater General has been a madhouse with dozens of sunstroke cases. Not just kids playing outside too long, either—people who should know better. Farmers and other folks who know what the sun and heat can do."

Danny smiled. "Today will be different, Julie. Let's make a deal: no discussing my job, your job, or the drought. Let's just float around on the pond and forget about everything."

"You've got a deal. No complaining, no whining." She held out her hand, and Danny took it. They shook pseudoformally to seal the agreement. Then, they both laughed.

After driving out to the Tozek farm, Julie pulled off the road in the same place she had almost two months ago, and they unloaded their horses. Danny worked the gate and closed it after they went through. Myron Tozek's land looked more desiccated and desolate than it had at their earlier visit. A feeble breeze that sprang up periodically was enough to raise dust devils of the dried soil that danced for a dozen feet or so before sifting back to earth when the wind deserted them. Both of the horses broke sweat almost immediately.

"I guess we walk these boys out and back," Julie commented. "Even a slow trot is too much for them today."

"Concentrate on how good that water's gonna feel. That'll make the half mile shorter," Danny said.

The pond had shrunk by about a quarter of its size since they'd last been there. The willows looked as if they'd gotten smaller too—their leaves a bit less green, and the rough grass around them moving toward brown. The tips of underwater weeds could be seen at the surface of the pond close to shore. The shore itself was a muted green in places where algae had gotten a start when the water receded. A group of teens on the far side of the pond looked listless too—they sprawled on towels lethargically, only three of them in the water.

Neither Danny nor Julie spoke for a minute.

"Sad, isn't it?" Danny finally said.

Julie forced a smile. "Different, is all."

Julie was the first into the water. The weeds close to shore scraped against her legs with a creepy, slimy sensation. When she was in up to her waist, she dove and stroked to the bottom. The layer of tepid water was deeper this time, but once again, closer to the bottom, the frigid springwater very pleasantly shocked her body. The abrupt transition from sweltering hot to winter cold was exhilarating, transforming. Suddenly, it seemed like a very fine afternoon.

She glanced over at Danny off to her side. He was smiling, a small section of his teeth showing through the clear water as he absorbed the sweet respite from the heat. He saw her looking at him and stuck his thumbs into his ears and wiggled his fingers at her, at the same time squinching

188

his face into a mask. Julie laughed, inhaled water, and had to push herself to the surface, where she gasped for air and continued laughing.

After swimming for a while, they got out to sit on their towels and have a snack. The milk container's solid ice had turned to a liquidy slush, but its temperature kept the bottles of springwater refreshingly cool. The bread was slightly soggy from condensation on the bottles that surrounded it but still retained a satisfying crunch. The cheddar was excellent.

Danny, leaning back on his towel, munched happily on cheese and bread. "This is the best gift I've gotten in a long time," he said.

"Gift?" Julie asked. "What're you talking about? It's just a throw-together snack."

"But," Danny announced, "today's my birthday. So—this stuff is a gift."

Julie sat stunned, a piece of cheese stopped halfway to her mouth. "Your birthday?" she asked incredulously. "Today's your birthday?"

Danny's smile began to slide away. "Well . . . yeah. It is."

Months of frustration with Danny's hot-and-cold behavior bubbled up out of Julie. Her voice trembled slightly as she spoke. "I have never come across a person as selfish and as closed off as you are, Danny."

"Selfish? I don't know what you're talking about! How have I been—"

"Yes, selfish!" Julie nearly shouted. "Don't you think hiding inside yourself, hiding away from people who care about

189

you, care for you, is selfish? You couldn't even tell me your birthday was coming up, could you? It would have been really terrible if I'd gone out and gotten you a gift—maybe even something you'd like. You couldn't let that happen—it'd mean you were actually letting another person into your life. No, that'd be impossible for you."

Danny's face looked as if he'd taken an unforeseeable slap. "Julie—c'mon," he protested weakly. "It's no big deal. Birthdays are for seven-year-olds. I didn't want you to go to any trouble."

Julie knew that holding back now would have been like trying to hold back an erupting volcano. "Maybe birthdays are for kids—but relationships are for adults! Did you ever stop to think that maybe I wanted to go through some trouble to do something nice for you? That I would've actually enjoyed it?" She shook her head. "Of course not! Why would you ever think about something that silly, that foolish? If you did, it might mean that you cared for someone, Danny—someone other than yourself."

Again she shook her head, but slowly this time, tears glinting in her eyes. "I've had it with you, Danny Pulver. I'm all finished playing your insane mind games. Find another woman to pretend with, 'cause I'm all done." Julie got to her feet and pulled her towel from the ground, tipping the rest of the food and the unopened bottles of water onto the dirt. "I'm leaving. Get your horse and I'll drop you home."

Danny stood slowly, looking very confused. "I . . . I really don't understand what all this is about. If I've done something to hurt you, I'm sorry—but I don't know what it is.

A stupid birthday? This doesn't make any sense. C'mon, honey, let's—"

The tone of Julie's voice and the fire behind her words were as sharp and stinging as a cut with a quirt. "Don't you call me honey unless you mean it!"

"Julie . . . I . . ."

But he was talking to her back. Julie stomped off to where she'd tied Drifter, tugged her jeans, boots, and T-shirt over her wet bathing suit, and swung onto her horse. Drifter, eyes wide and ears pricked, danced in place, picking up on Julie's wrath. She reined his head around and set off at a lope toward her truck and trailer, regardless of the heat and the penetrating clutches of the sun. Only after her horse broke a heavy sweat did Julie check him to a walk.

Drifter was loaded into the trailer and Julie behind the truck's steering wheel staring straight ahead when Danny reached the road. He led Dakota into the trailer, secured the rear gate, and climbed into the passenger seat.

"Look," he said as Julie drove away from the shoulder, "I'd like to—"

"Not now, Danny," Julie answered without looking at him. "I just can't talk to you right now."

"I don't understand what . . ." He stopped and let the sentence die. Julie felt his eyes on her face as she drove. "Whatever," Danny said, resignation and now a touch of defensiveness in his voice.

That was the last word spoken between them. Julie stopped at the mouth of Danny's driveway; he left the cab and slammed the door, unloaded Dakota, and closed the gate.

Julie drove off. Her eyes flicked to her rearview mirror. Danny wasn't watching her as she left—he was leading his horse to the pasture gate.

The road shimmered for a moment in Julie's vision, but after she wiped her eyes on her arm, the problem was gone.

The trailer wasn't going anywhere overnight, Julie decided. The backing and maneuvering of it into its place was more trouble than she cared to undertake just then. She eased Drifter down the ramp and put him in the stall she'd prepared that morning. He still had some sweat on his hide so she worked him over with a grain sack, for once ignoring his grunts of pleasure.

I've known Danny for almost three years—and I don't know him at all. It wasn't the birthday. It was everything. I was right. He's selfish and closed into himself and barricaded away from me and everyone else in the real world. It was time for this to happen. In fact, what took place today—what I said—was long, long overdue.

"Hollow," she said aloud to the silence in her kitchen as she sat at the table. "I feel hollow." Her eyes wandered about the room, stopping on the open cupboard next to the sink, where the side of an economy-sized bag of Milk-Bones was visible. Sunday appeared in her mind. *I'm not going to allow myself to do this,* she chided herself. *It's counterproductive. Why mourn over a guy who was never really there? I have options, I have a good life, and I have . . . options.*

Julie got up from her chair, stepped to the cupboard,

and closed it quietly but firmly. The wall phone was only a couple of steps away. She looked at it for what seemed like a long time. She took the few steps and stood in front of the telephone. Her right hand moved toward the receiver slowly, as if she were lifting a weight. She put her index finger on the little lever and pulled it into the off position, silencing the ringer. Any calls that came in would go to her recorder—she could listen to them or skip past them or delete them tomorrow or whenever she cared to. There was a finality to the hushed click of the lever that brought a lump to her throat. She went to her purse, removed her cell phone, and keyed in the call transfer command, sending incoming calls to her home number. Then she crossed the kitchen and sat again at the table.

A thought—or perhaps it was more of an image—insinuated itself into her mind. Julie saw herself as a whining, demanding woman who insisted on running not only her own life but the lives of the people she cared about. The image made her cringe.

Is that what I'm doing? Have I built this silly birthday thing into a monumental statement that Danny never intended?

Julie began to rise but sat down again. Her mind raced. *What have I done? Have I hissy-fitted myself out of the life of the best guy I've ever met?*

The next few days were difficult. Julie went through her home chores and her work obligations competently, even carefully, but without feeling, without emotion.

This is the way a robot feels, she thought, not missing the point that robots, by definition, have no feelings. *I did the right thing, the only thing I could do. I couldn't live like that any longer. At least now I don't have to wonder about Danny Pulver and his feelings—or his lack of them. Better now than later. Better the hurt than waiting for something that would never happen, hoping it would but also knowing that it wouldn't. Pain goes away. Maybe I overreacted—but maybe I didn't.*

That weekend—five days after she'd gone to Tozek's pond with Danny—Julie sat outside her kitchen in a lawn chair, drinking iced tea and listening halfheartedly to a news show on her transistor radio. The crunch of tires on the stones in her driveway pulled her to her feet just as the gleaming snout of Ken's cruiser eased behind the house. She was genuinely pleased to see him. When she'd played her answering machine tape back the day before, there had been a "just wanted to say hi" call from him. She hadn't returned the call yet.

Ken stopped behind the house and shut off his engine but kept his radio operating. "On duty," he smiled as Julie approached the car. "I don't want to miss a call."

Julie stood at the driver's window. "Good to see you, Ken."

"Good to see you too. You busy?"

Julie smiled. "Not at the moment. What brings you by when you're on duty?"

The smile left his face. "Actually," he said, "I'm here on business tonight. Both yours and mine. Can you get in the car for a minute? I really don't want to leave my radio."

Intrigued, Julie walked around the car to the passenger

side. Ken leaned across the bench seat and shoved the door open. Julie settled in and met Ken's eyes. "What's up?"

"I think . . ." He hesitated. "I think I have a story for you. A big one. But I don't want to put you on the spot. And I certainly don't want to louse up what's becoming a great relationship."

"It has been good," Julie agreed carefully. "But I have no idea what you're talking about—the story for me, I mean."

"Do you want to hear about it? It'd have to be totally confidential for a short time, but there's no one in the world I'd rather see write the story when it breaks. Like I said, it's a big one."

"Of course I'm interested. It's my job to be interested. But if there's a confidentiality issue, maybe this isn't something I should be involved in."

"It is an issue, but just for a little while longer. Everything is pretty much in place. A few days and the whole mess can go public. Can you trust me on that?"

"If you can trust me to keep whatever this is quiet until you give me the go-ahead. I admit I'm interested—*intrigued* may be a better word."

"OK," Ken said. He reached under the seat of his car and pulled out an eight-by-ten-inch manila envelope. "My PI skills are apparently still in good shape," he said, "and so is the little Nikon I used back then. Take a look." He handed the envelope to Julie.

She opened the clasp and withdrew several black-and-white photographs. The first one showed Chief of Police Ross Craig standing next to a pair of bikers. The cyclists were

Hell's Angels types, hairy, dirty, their bare arms covered with tattoos. One of them was holding a paper-wrapped package about the size of a brick, obviously handing it to the chief.

The second photo was a grainy night shot of Ross Craig entering the back door of the Bulldogger and carrying a large briefcase. Rick Castle held the door open from the inside.

9

Julie flipped through the rest of the pictures. They were more of the same: Craig with the bikers, Castle and Craig together behind the Bulldogger, Craig's personal car—a new Buick—with Castle removing a package from its open trunk.

"You've been busy, Ken," Julie said.

"Those packages contain methamphetamines. Craig is crooked, and I can prove it."

"How? These photos are good, but I don't know that alone they can establish that something illegal's going on. Or can they? You're the expert here."

"You're right," Ken said. "Taken alone, the pictures don't tell the whole story. But what happened last night does. Craig dropped one of the packages on the pavement behind the Bulldogger, and it wasn't wrapped well. Some of the powder was left on the pavement. I have that on film that I haven't developed yet. I used a Chem-Kit and tested the powder I scraped up later. It was positive for meth. I called in a Montana state trooper friend, and he tested it too, with the same result."

"Whew. Sounds like you've got it covered. What's going to happen next?"

"Surveillance until the next delivery. Then, we grab Craig, Castle, and a few others from inside the bar—the bartender for one, and some of the losers who hang there for questioning."

"Whew," Julie repeated. "Look—I promised confidentiality, but there's something else you should know." She took a breath. "Nancy—my boss at the *News-Express*—has been looking at Ross Craig for a couple of months. I don't know what she has, but I think you need to talk to her."

"I'll certainly do that. There's no such thing as a case that's too strong."

"There's one other thing," Julie continued. "Craig pulled me over a few months ago on a phony broken taillight bit. He warned me away from the Bulldogger and from Rick Castle. I didn't do anything about it then . . ."

"Why didn't you come to me about it?"

"I don't know. I guess I figured it was just better to lay low. I knew Nancy was looking at him—and I figured it was just Craig showing me how big and tough he was. Now, with what you've found out, it's all different."

"Yeah. It sure is." He thought for a moment. "Would you testify about what happened that day?"

"In a heartbeat."

Ken nodded. "A trial could get messy. I'm sure Craig and Castle will get some heavy legal representation to try to beat this thing. They'll try to make you look like a miffed reporter out to get a sensational story."

"I guess I wouldn't be much of a journalist—or much of a person, for that matter—if I let some lawyer scare me off." She thought for a moment. "But I need your permission to discuss what you've told me and shown me with Nancy Lewis."

"I don't see a problem with that, unless . . ."

A hiss of static from the cruiser's radio was followed by a voice stating something Julie couldn't understand. Ken grabbed the microphone from the dashboard.

"Dispatch. Four-ten."

Julie was able to pick up the words "in progress" among the number codes from the dispatcher, but that was all.

"Ten-four," Ken said. He turned to her. "Gotta run, Julie. Will you be up at 11:30 or so? I'll be off at 11:00, and we need to talk a little more."

"I'll be up. See you then," Julie said as she opened her door hurriedly and stepped out of the car.

Ken didn't waste any time responding to the radio call. His tires hurled cinders and dirt as he sped down the driveway, and they screeched over the howl of his engine when he reached the road. In a moment, his siren began whooping.

When the night was quiet again, Julie went into her kitchen and took her place at the table.

He knows how important this story could be to the News-Express. *It would go statewide and quite possibly hit the nationals. It'd be the biggest feature since Nancy came on board—and the most important story I've ever written. Ken took a big chance on me. If I run my mouth off too soon, he'll be certain to lose a job he loves. Handing over investigations of pending cases to reporters isn't something cops do if they want to keep working in law enforcement.*

She got up and walked to the counter. Preparing a pot of coffee had as much to do with keeping her hands busy as actually wanting a cup.

Would I risk my job to help Ken Townsend? The coffee was perking, but Julie was too lost in her internal monologue to pay any attention to it. *Probably not, unless . . . unless what? How do I feel about Ken? He's important to me—perhaps much more important than he realizes. He's good to me. He cares about me, and I think he could love me.*

Is Danny on my mind too much for me to really think straight about Ken? I've known Danny for more than three years and Ken for a few months. But—so what? I've known Louie Sciortino at Louie's Market longer than I've known Danny, and I wouldn't want to spend the rest of my life with Louie. Julie couldn't help smiling at that thought.

Butcher Leaves Wife of 40 Years
For Wimpy, Indecisive Reporter

Her laugh brought her back to her kitchen. She poured a cup of coffee and took it outside and turned her lawn chair to face directly west. The sun was setting with a wave of such vivid color across the horizon that the sight pushed Danny, Ken, and the Craig story out of her mind. The colors were so rich and opulent that she could almost taste them.

The respite was a welcome one, but it was too short to offer Julie any real relief. The men in her life again took over her thoughts as she sat in the burgeoning darkness with her cup of coffee cooling and forgotten in her hand.

Almost a week had passed since the day at the pond. Danny hadn't called or come to see her. Wasn't that a perfect indication of his feelings toward her? Didn't that tell her that she was better off without him? And wasn't it true that she'd had more than a passing interest in Ken since the day she met him?

Still . . . I really laid into Danny last week. Maybe he's feeling that I've completely shut the door on him, on anything that could happen between us. She shook her head slightly, ruefully. *The eternal question all modern women seem to end up facing at one time or another: should I call him, talk with him, see what can be salvaged? Maybe so,* she admitted to herself. After a moment, she added the thought, *Not maybe so—definitely so. But not this minute, not right now. Soon, but not right now.*

Julie carried her coffee inside and dumped it in the sink. She wandered to her living room and clicked on her old TV set. As usual, there was nothing worth watching—or at least nothing that caught her attention enough to pull her out of her brooding. She turned the set off and stretched out on the couch to stare up at the ceiling.

"Julie?" a voice suddenly called from outside the kitchen door. "Julie? You here?"

She straightened quickly and swung her feet to the floor. "Come on in, Ken—I'm in the living room." She ran her hands through her hair, which seemed to have formed into a sort of flying wedge on the right side. She sighed.

Ken came into the room. He'd changed out of his uniform and looked good in jeans, a polo shirt, and western boots.

"I must've dozed off," Julie said a bit groggily. "What time is it?"

"Twenty after eleven." He looked closely at her. "What happened to your hair?" It was easy enough to see that he was trying to swallow a smile.

Julie leaped up from the couch and dashed up the stairs to the bathroom. "You're never supposed to say 'What happened to your hair?' to a woman!" she called over her shoulder.

"I didn't mean that it was unattractive," Ken called up the steps. "I just . . ."

She kicked the bathroom door shut as she dragged her brush through her hair and giggled at her image in the mirror. *Even when he's teasing me, this guy makes me laugh.*

When Julie came down the stairs, Ken was still standing, not pacing but obviously tense. Julie crossed the room to the couch and sat. "Sit, Ken—you're nervous enough to make me nervous."

"Yeah. I know it." He walked to the love seat adjacent to the couch and dropped into it. In a moment, he was on his feet again, and looked as if he were about to fly apart.

"What is it? Was that call you got a bad one? I've never seen you so—"

"No—it sounded like trouble from the dispatcher, but when I got there it was a couple of kids throwing off leftover firecrackers from the Fourth of July. It was called in to the PD as gunfire."

"OK, then," Julie said. "We need to talk about what we discussed earlier."

Ken started pacing the floor. "Everything's in place. The day after tomorrow Craig is supposed to bring in another haul. We've had an undercover sliding in and out of the Bulldogger, and he's sure of it. Craig and Castle and those other punks are going down." He stopped in front of Julie and met her eyes. "I know I'm like a kid on Christmas Eve, but I want this very badly. There's something about a dirty cop that makes me sick."

"Of course you want it, Ken—so do I. Sit down, OK? Tell me how you managed to put this thing together."

Ken sat on the edge of the love seat. "I figured out early that there was something wrong about Craig. I saw his Blazer behind the Bulldogger a few times while I was on patrol. He just bought a new Bass-Buster fishing boat that he's been keeping under a cover behind his garage. I checked with the dealer. He paid cash. That's kind of hard to do on a cop's pay in Coldwater—even on a chief's pay. Plus, he's driving that new Buick—says it's his wife's—even though he has use of the cruiser assigned to him. I suppose it's remotely possible that he saved up the money or inherited it or something, but I can't buy that at all."

Ken's gaze fixed on Julie as he spoke. "I started to follow Craig during some of my off hours. I'm very good as a tail—good enough so that even a longtime cop wouldn't be aware that he was being followed. I saw Craig meet with the bikers a couple of times, and I got the pictures I showed you. The big thing, of course, is actually catching these guys in the act, and we'll do that."

Ken smiled. "In fact, we'll be doing it on camera. A trooper is going to be in that warehouse that backs up to the rear of the Bulldogger with a video setup."

"I've *got* to be there, Ken—with the video guy."

Again, Ken smiled. "Somehow, I knew you'd say that. It's safe—I wouldn't even talk to you about it if it weren't. I talked to the team, and they agree that having a press person there to observe and to write the story would lock the whole thing up perfectly. So—you're on the team."

Julie's mind raced. "I've got to talk to Nancy first thing tomorrow. I can't just go ahead with this without informing her. But Ken—this is a terrific opportunity for me and for the *News-Express*. Thanks."

"Sure. I wouldn't have it any other way—especially after Craig's attempt to intimidate you. This could be very big for me too, you know."

"What do you mean?"

Ken broke eye contact and suddenly seemed to find the floor directly in front of him very interesting. "I can't say any more at this point about that," he said.

"OK, that's fine." She stood. "It's kind of late for coffee, but I have iced tea and diet soda. Can I get you anything?"

Ken glanced at his watch. "No thanks—I'm on days starting tomorrow, and 5:30 comes awfully early. Walk me out to my car?"

It was a starlit night with a three-quarter moon. Ken took Julie's hand as they walked to the cruiser. His palm felt good against hers. A coyote yelped off to the east somewhere, but beyond that, the night was silent—and, of course, hot.

Rather than opening his door, Ken leaned against it, still holding Julie's hand. "Well . . ." he said. "Good night, Julie." He didn't release her hand.

"'Night, Ken," Julie said quietly.

Then, they were kissing—not hungrily and not quickly, but almost in slow motion. They each stepped forward half a step, and Ken put his arm around Julie's shoulders as her free hand found the back of his neck and her fingers moved through his hair. It was a warm and gentle kiss, close and sweet and innocent.

They separated as slowly as they'd come together. There was no embarrassment and no self-consciousness to the moment. It was their first kiss together and seemed to Julie to be a culmination of the good times, the long talks, the mutual trust they'd shared. Ken released her hand, touched her face with his fingertips for the briefest of moments, and opened his door. The huge engine muttered to life, and the cruiser backed away from Julie.

"You should've told me about Craig stopping you, Julie," Nancy Lewis said. Her desk, as usual, was bare except for her prized Mt. Blanc fountain pen and a fresh legal pad.

"I know you're right," Julie said. "But that was the same day you told me Craig and Castle were off limits to me. I documented the whole traffic stop because I knew that I'd need to tell you about it eventually. I guess . . . well, I guess

I thought it was a big-frog, small-pond thing. Craig showing me what a macho supercop he was. As a journalist, I
should've known better." After a couple of seconds she added,
"But there was no way in the world I could prove that it
actually happened. My word against the chief of police."

Nancy's telephone buzzed. She punched a button and
said, "Please, Elisha—no calls until Julie and I are finished.
Thanks." She replaced the receiver.

"Valid point," Nancy allowed. "Officer Townsend called
me late last night—very late—and we talked about what's
happening," she said. "I'll admit that I might have thought
he was a disgruntled new-hire, a guy who didn't like his boss.
Then he told me about the pictures and the involvement
of the troopers and the takedown scheduled for tomorrow
night." She leaned back in her chair. "Incidentally, Officer Townsend didn't mention Craig stopping you. Even
so, Townsend's information filled in some holes in what
I've developed through my sources over the last couple of
months. It's abundantly clear that Ross Craig is selling drugs
he buys from that motorcycle gang through Rick Castle
and the Bulldogger."

"Being caught in the act will put the lid on the whole
affair," Julie pointed out. "That's why it's important that I
be there, Nancy—in the warehouse with the video guy."

Nancy sighed. "These things can fall apart in a big hurry.
We're not dealing with nice people here. I don't know . . ."

Julie leaned forward toward Nancy. "Thanks to you, we
have terrific Internet access. Lexis-Nexis, all that. When the
system was first up, I ran your name. Several years ago, when

you were still a reporter, you went undercover and bought an African lion from a bunch of un-nice people who were importing protected animals illegally and—"

Nancy laughed heartily, and her face colored the slightest bit. "I haven't thought about that story in years," she said. "The paper I was writing for had me accompany the lion back to Africa, where he was set free. Great story," she mused.

"This will be a great story too," Julie said. "My point is that—"

Nancy waved away whatever Julie's point was. "I need your word that you'll stay in that room in the warehouse with the cop until everything is over. Agreed?"

"Agreed."

"And get the copy to me as soon as you've written it. I'll be right here in my office waiting for you." She laughed. "I haven't used the word *scoop* in years—but that's exactly what this story will be."

"I feel like Lois Lane at the *Daily Planet*," Julie admitted.

Nancy raised an eyebrow. "Does that make Ken Townsend Superman?"

In her truck in the parking lot that morning, Julie started her engine, turned the air-conditioning on full blast, and concentrated on breathing and exhaling deeply and slowly. Strangely, the exhilaration she'd experienced in Nancy's office—the heady taste of accomplishment— seemed to diminish in the short walk through the steaming lot. She felt down, almost sad, for some reason she didn't understand.

What is this? she demanded of herself. *It's a great story, and I can tell Nancy is as excited about bringing down that crooked cop as I am. What then . . .*

Ken.

It's Ken. Last night was good, kissing him was good. He respects me and he cares for me, probably deeply. And he's as much as a woman could want in a man.

Then why am I feeling like this?

The answer didn't come to Julie as she plodded through her day. She was two pieces ahead on her drought series. That didn't mean she couldn't work on another of the articles—but it did mean she was under no time obligation to do so. She tidied her home and loaded her washing machine. She paid a few bills, rearranged her sock and underwear drawer, and ran her vacuum cleaner.

In her office Julie had a running list of telephone calls she needed to place to verify or repudiate information she'd developed, to clarify points she planned to make in articles, and to interview people who were peripheral to her stories but could, perhaps, provide fresh insight into her topic. She sighed. It wasn't that she didn't enjoy speaking to people or accomplishing interviews; rather, it was the interminable time she spent on hold, listening to sappy music—or, worse, canned advertising—that irritated her like fingernails screeching across a blackboard.

She settled herself at her desk with a fresh mug of coffee and tapped in the first number on her list—a professor of ecological studies at Montana State University. A perky secretary asked her to hold for the professor. There was a click, and then a string section began destroying the old sixties rock anthem "Sittin' on the Dock of the Bay." After several minutes a headline appeared in her mind:

**Telephone Receiver Fuses to Ear of Reporter—
Medical Insurance Refuses to Pay for Surgery**

The song ended and the strings section launched into "The Age of Aquarius." Mercifully, the professor came on. He was pleased to speak with Julie, wanted to know if he'd be quoted in the article, and spelled his name twice. He didn't tell Julie anything she didn't already know, but she took down a good quote line from him on her legal pad.

She encountered answering machines on her next two calls, and she left a message each time.

A dust bowl/westward migration authority in Oklahoma who'd recently had a nonfiction work titled *The Sweet Promise of California—And the Bitter Reality* made Julie's telephone time and frustration more than worthwhile. The woman was knowledgeable, articulate—and genuinely fascinating. Julie felt a bit guilty when she glanced at her clock and saw that she'd kept the historian on the line for fifty minutes. But she'd filled three pages on her pad with notes.

She refilled her coffee mug and attacked her list once again.

❧

At 8:30 Julie was in her lawn chair outside her kitchen, watching the end of another spectacular sunset. The flagrantly beautiful colors across the western sky calmed her a bit, at least partially put things in perspective. She sipped a Diet Pepsi. Her thoughts were more ordered, more logical—and more painful.

There's only one thing wrong with Ken, but it's a monumental problem, she admitted to herself. *If I'd met him four years ago I'd probably be his wife right now. But I didn't meet him then.*

The problem with Ken is that he's not Danny Pulver.

❧

The muted clang of steel horseshoes on the road rang into Julie's thoughts. It was full dark, and she wondered who would be riding at that time of night. There was a horse-crazy teen a few miles away who'd just bought a nice mare from Maggie, Julie recalled. *That's probably her. But riding at night on a road . . .*

The whirlwind at her feet told her who the rider was. Sunday licked at her hands, her face, any part he could reach. His tail slapped her legs as he spun and patted at her knees with his forepaws.

Julie hugged the big, ecstatic dog. "Whatta great boy! Whatta gooooood dog! I'm so happy to see you!"

The collie's whining, deep from within his chest, was somehow mournful yet joyful at the same time.

Danny, on Dakota, rode around the corner of Julie's home and drew rein in front of her. "I was kind of hoping you'd be as happy to see me as you are to see Sunday," he said. He stepped down from his horse's back and stood next to Dakota, his hand on the animal's neck.

"This is . . . a surprise," Julie said, rising from her lawn chair.

"Yeah. I'm sure it is. A good surprise?"

Julie could smell the light sweat of Dakota and—almost imperceptibly—the good cologne Danny wore. He was in jeans and his western boots and a short-sleeved work shirt that had been washed many times.

"May I put this guy in an empty stall? I'll leave him saddled—just loosen the cinch a bit," Danny said.

"Sure. Give him some water and a flake of hay. You know where everything is." *It's not Dakota who broke my heart, after all.*

Danny led his horse through the darkness to the barn. In a moment, the outside light came on. Julie heard the smooth sliding sound of the big front door being opened, and then the central aisle fluorescents flickered and came to life. Drifter huffed at the disturbance, and Dakota snorted back.

Julie swallowed hard several times. She wasn't sure what she wanted to do—leap up and run away from Danny's mind games or stay where she was and be duped into another few years of frustration.

He deserves a chance to say what he wants to say.

"It's been a while, Dan," Julie said carefully, controlling

211

her voice so that there was no perceptible emotion in it, as if she were asking a grocer where the canned peas were located.

"Yeah. It has been. Too long."

Julie sat down. "Grab the other lawn chair if you like."

Danny unfolded the chair that had been leaning against the house and placed it a few feet from Julie. He settled into the chair, but even in the murky darkness he gave the impression of tension, as if he were a tightly coiled spring. "I've been thinking a lot," he said.

"So have I, Danny."

"You're still angry with me."

Julie didn't respond.

"What happened wasn't about my birthday," he said.

"No."

"You've been seeing a lot of Ken Townsend, haven't you?"

"Is there any reason why I shouldn't spend time with Ken? Whatever it was that was going on between us seems to have ended, hasn't it?"

Danny nodded. "Seems that way."

The silence was as thick and uncomfortable as the heat—heavy, tense, pervasive.

Danny sighed. "Suppose you let me talk for a bit, Julie, and you just listen. I need to say what I've got to say, and I've given it so much thought I just about have my speech memorized. Would that be OK?"

Julie nodded.

Danny began to stand but thought better of it and remained in his chair. His eyes found Julie's. "A few years ago," he began, "you might recall that I was courting Maggie quite seriously. I was in love with her. Maybe I'm a late bloomer or just slow or whatever, but Maggie was the first woman I was genuinely in love with. I guess I was too busy in high school with my car and working and in college with my pre-vet and veterinary studies. So, anyway, Maggie was my first serious romance."

He was silent for several moments. "Of course, Maggie chose Ian. I couldn't be happier for both of them now. That's what I said at the time too." He cleared his throat needlessly before going on. "I was flat-out lying about that. A man doesn't stop loving a woman simply because she marries someone else. It doesn't work that way. I was angry and hurt and heartsick, Julie, and it didn't go away." He shook his head, and his smile was a sad one. "Even at their wedding I half believed that Maggie was going to turn away from Ian and run to me like what's-her-name in *The Graduate*."

"Danny—I'm really sorry. I had no idea that—"

"Please, Julie. Just listen."

Julie swallowed. "OK."

"I let what I was feeling turn into bitterness. I was sure I'd never be happy and never find a woman who could be trusted. The thing is, it—my bitterness—happened slowly, and I guess I wasn't completely aware of it.

"Then there was you, Julie. I . . . fell in love with you. I mean that completely and totally. But I was still carrying my past and my bitterness, and I couldn't—didn't—tell you what was going on with me. That's over now."

"What's over?"

Danny's voice became slightly louder and more forceful. "The hiding of my feelings, my building of walls—that's over. That's what I mean. I promise you that—if you can consider letting me into your life again."

"I don't know what to say, Danny," Julie said, her voice trembling.

Danny stood and took a step closer to Julie. "I understand. I didn't expect an immediate answer. Just let me say one more thing, and I'll get my horse and leave. I love you, Julie. I want to spend the rest of my life with you. I'll prove to you that being away from you has changed me, made me realize how precious you are. All I ask is that you give me some time with you to prove everything I've said. I'm here, Julie. All you need to do is to let me know that you'll give me a chance." He turned away and walked toward the barn.

Julie didn't follow him. She just sat there with her thoughts whirling in her mind, trying to believe what she'd just heard.

Within a few minutes Danny led Dakota out of the barn, slid the door shut, and swung into his saddle. Julie could see the patches of white on the horse's coat and Sunday's white chest in the dark, but Danny's face was unclear. He put Dakota into a quick walk, and Julie listened until she could no longer hear the hoofbeats.

10

"Like the inside of a pizza oven in here," Julie mumbled to herself as she made her way through the main floor of the warehouse. Even in the full midday power of the sun, the lighting in the building was dismal. The few windows in the steel fabricated structure were thickly coated with dust and dead insects. The place was huge and as silent as a funeral parlor at midnight. Much of the first floor was taken up by pallets of various appliances in cardboard cartons, piled pallet upon pallet to within inches of the twenty-foot ceiling. The paths between the pallets didn't seem wide enough to allow room to maneuver the forklifts that stacked the appliances, but obviously they were.

The occasional forklift, still and silent, hulked in the murky darkness like some sort of sleeping prehistoric beast. Julie walked in the center of an aisle of seemingly endless stacks of washing machines, dryers, refrigerators, and ranges. She could barely see the penciled map Ken had prepared for her, but she knew she was looking for a stairway at the far end of the warehouse that led to the second floor of the building.

Abruptly, the appliance area ended. Now the pallets held machine parts—what sort of machines, Julie had no idea.

The silence and the heat were both oppressive and a little bit frightening. She found it disquieting to be alone in a place where there was almost a total absence of sound, except for the soles of her boots slapping the concrete floor.

It wasn't quite noon, but nobody knew exactly when Craig would be making his delivery. Ken had learned that the chief was scheduled to meet with the city council from 9:00 a.m. until noon and then to have lunch with them, so a morning drop-off wasn't likely. Outlaw bikers weren't known for keeping early morning hours, anyway. But the police were taking no chances. The video man had been in place since 9:00, and the unmarked state trooper vehicles had been in position on the side streets around the Bulldogger—with two pickups in the bar's parking lot—since 10:00.

The steel steps of the stairway to the second floor were almost ladder steep. Julie climbed carefully, the palm of her hand sweating against the stair rail. Skylights in the ceiling provided more light than what existed downstairs. There were a few offices on the second floor. A series of desks, credenzas, and filing cabinets clustered in front of the offices.

Julie tapped lightly on the closed door of an office with the name Rich Novack stenciled on it.

"Come in," a masculine voice sounded from inside.

Julie had anticipated TV-broadcast-sized video equipment and was surprised to see a unit about the size of a brick mounted on a tripod at the dingy window that faced the rear of the Bulldogger. A small, closed-circuit TV monitor sat on the desk, along with a control pad that allowed the

216

technician to adjust the view of the camera without himself appearing in the window.

"I'm assuming you're Julie Downs," the tech said with a smile. "If you're not, I've got a problem here."

"I'm Julie." She walked to where the tech was sitting in an armed office chair with his elbows on the desk in front of him, looking out the window. He looked more like a disoriented hippie than a cop or police technician. His shoulder-length hair could have used a long and thorough shampoo, and his jeans were threadbare and grease-spotted. He wore a leather vest over his tanned upper body, without a shirt or T-shirt.

"I've been the night watchman here for a couple weeks," he said. "This place pays next to nothing, and I look like the sort who'll work for wages like that." He extended his hand. "Tom Davis, Montana State Police."

Julie shook Tom's hand. "There's no one else here? No business going on?"

"Hasn't been for almost a month," Tom said. "Most of the stuff here is under receivership from a couple of bankrupt appliance stores, and none of it is going anywhere for a while. I've been more or less living here—folks are used to seeing me ride up on my bike and use my key to get in at various times of day."

"What about the workers, the office staff?"

Tom shook his head. "Laid off. Some of the grunts are on call if they're needed, but that's about it. Kind of a trickle-down effect from the drought. Businesses are dropping all over the place." He looked at Julie's purse. "I hope you brought a book with you. I don't think anything's going to happen until the joint closes. This could be a long day for you."

"I never thought to bring a book along," Julie admitted.

Tom hooked a carton from under the desk with his foot. The carton was overflowing with paperbacks. "Take a look through these if you like. They're mostly novels—westerns, cops, action-adventure—with a couple of true crime books and a couple of poetry collections. Help yourself to anything you find. Like I said, it could be a long day."

Julie started toward the books.

"Whoa!" Tom held up his hand. "Don't walk in front of the window," he said. "That's about the only rule here—that and no lights after it gets dark. There's enough light from the security lights to read after dark. It's not likely that anyone from the Bulldogger will be looking up here, but if they do, we don't want to tip them off."

"Sorry." Julie smiled. "I should've thought of that." She ducked below the window and looked through the books. She picked out a paperback Ed McBain 87th Precinct mystery and a collection of *Far Side* cartoons by Gary Larson.

"I've been following your drought series in the *News-Express*," Tom said. "It's good stuff—great writing."

"Thanks, Tom. That's always good to hear."

"When Ken first asked about having you here I vetoed it right away." He smiled somewhat abashedly. "Actually, what I said was to the effect of, 'I don't need some reporter looking for a story in here and getting in my way.' Then Ken told me who you are and what you've been doing."

Julie laughed. "I promise not to stick my nose in where it doesn't belong."

Tom laughed too. "Good," he said. "You know, Ken pretty much put this whole thing together on his own time, from the suspicions he had about the chief. And he did some good tailing too. I don't know that I could've followed Ross well enough so that he wouldn't pick up on the tail."

"He told me a bit about his PI experience," Julie said. "He said that's where he learned to follow a subject on foot or in a car without being observed."

"This bust—if it goes down as we think it will—could be really good for him. He's an excellent cop with lots of skills rookies take years to develop—if they ever do develop. He won't be in the bag for long. That's a sure thing."

"In the bag?" Julie asked.

"Uniform. Cop talk."

Julie took her books and sat on the floor near the window, her back against the wall. A small reciprocating fan Tom had set up on a chair didn't do much more than move the super-heated air around, but it was better than nothing. She began reading the mystery novel.

An hour later Tom passed Julie a bottle of chilled water from a small cooler next to his chair. "I got some sandwiches too, if you want. Oh—Ken left something for you." He delved back into the cooler and tossed her a giant-sized Snickers bar that was wonderfully cold.

"What a guy." She smiled for a moment, but then the smile faded.

What about Danny? Are his promises good? Is what he said

219

last night about loving me—wanting to spend his life with me—real? Or did he simply get lonely and have a change of heart that won't last?

She closed her book and held it in her lap. *Ken—with his Snickers bar and his kindness. With the way he seems to understand me, to know what I'm feeling—the way he makes me laugh. He's a good, good man.*

The clicking and whirring of the old classroom-type clock on the wall marked the passing of time. Julie found it was a good idea to stop glancing at it. She'd look once, read or think some more, and check the clock again, finding that perhaps five or six minutes had passed.

After what seemed like several eons, the sun began to recede. Julie ate the few remaining scraps of her candy bar. When the night security lights came on, they startled her from a light doze. Her throat was dry, and she needed a restroom.

"Could I bum another bottle of water? And is there a bathroom on this floor?"

Tom, as alert as ever, tossed Julie a bottle of springwater. "Just past the offices on the right-hand side."

Julie stood up and stretched. "You do surveillance well, Tom. The waiting doesn't seem to bother you."

"This one's easy. Once, I was sitting in a car I couldn't leave for two shifts because my relief couldn't get to me. But this . . . hey! What was that?"

Julie lowered the water bottle from her mouth and listened intently. She could hear a deep, low, faraway rumbling sound. Tom's and Julie's eyes met. "Was it thunder?" Julie asked, not quite believing it.

"I dunno. There wasn't any lightning that I could see. It might have been a jet breaking the sound barrier. There's an Air Force base not far from here, right?"

"There is, but it didn't sound like a sonic boom to me. Let's hope it was thunder."

On the way back from the ladies room Julie felt rather than heard the sound again. It was the slightest bit louder this time, and it set up minute vibrations in the floor of the steel building. A surge of anticipation, of energy, ran through her, and she hurried back to the surveillance point. "Lightning?" she asked.

"I didn't see any, but it could be behind us. We're facing west, and it could be a storm approaching from the east. I'm sure it wasn't a jet. It must've been thunder."

"Let's keep our fingers crossed," Julie said. "This could be a big night in more than one way. I hate to get my hopes up, but . . . well . . . I don't think I've heard thunder in a couple of years." She sat on the floor again, eyes focused on the window where the video camera was mounted. Tom, she noticed, had put his book aside and was concentrating on the window too.

Nothing happened for a long, tedious hour. Then a jagged, hissing streak of pure white light seemed to illuminate the entire world. Julie gasped as the lightning flickered and the light strobed in the office. The crash of the thunder was louder than a cannon, a slamming, manic explosion that shredded the silence of the evening.

221

The first rain struck the window like handfuls of hurled pebbles; the drops fell sharply on the glass, power-washing away the accumulated dust and grit and running it down the window surface in brownish rivulets that were quickly replaced by clean streams.

Julie was transfixed as she moved closer to the window. She watched the rain as if it were a deluge of tiny, precious diamonds, and felt a monumental sense of relief and an ecstatic sort of joy that brought tears to her eyes.

"It's been so long," she murmured to herself.

Tom turned in his chair away from the monitor and angled to the window, watching the rain as raptly as Julie. Neither Julie nor Tom spoke for several long minutes, until the initial cloudburst settled into a more constant, life-giving downpour. Finally, Julie asked, "What time is it, Tom?"

"Um—9:47. Why?"

"Because I plan on saying in print, 'On this date at 9:47 p.m., the first appreciable rain in over one and a half years broke the back of the drought that had held a large part of the state of Montana in its grasp.'"

The rain continued, strongly but not aggressively, with a drenching, constant cacophony against the metal roof of the warehouse. Julie imagined she could hear the soil welcoming the rain, drinking it down, drawing life from it.

"Julie—lookit this," Tom called to her, pointing to his monitor.

Julie stood and crossed the office to stand behind Tom. A pair of teens—a boy and a girl—had apparently been cross-ing behind the Bulldogger and now stood holding hands, looking up into the sky and letting the rain drench them. The girl's long hair was lank and dripping and their clothing was sopping wet, but still they stood celebrating.

"I know exactly how those kids feel," Tom mused.

"Me too," Julie breathed. "Me too."

Another pair of hours passed, and the rain continued unabated, as if making up for the long absence. Julie, back on the floor and leaning against the wall, stared at the hypnotic patterns on the window and sifted through her thoughts.

I know what I have to do. I don't want to hurt him, but I know what I have to do. I wish there were some way to—

"Showtime!" Tom announced.

Julie scurried to his side and stared at the monitor. A Buick—Ross Craig's personal car—had eased around the corner of the Bulldogger and stopped next to the back door of the bar. Tom clicked on the radio and keyed his microphone.

"Outpost one," he said tensely. "It's happening. Units hold and be ready to roll on my signal."

There were two men in the Buick. Another car—a beat-up station wagon—stopped behind Craig's car. The rain pattered on the sheet metal of the two vehicles. Nothing happened for several moments. The bleat of a horn barely reached the office. The back door of the bar opened a foot or so, and a shaggy head peered out. The door closed. Two men climbed out of the station wagon, one on either side of it, and stood in the rain, their backs to the Bulldogger. One cradled a shotgun. The other held a long-barreled pistol at his side.

"Units hold," Davis said. "Be ready."

The back door opened again, and Rick Castle stepped out of it. The trunk of Ross Craig's Buick popped open, and then Craig exited the car, walking to the rear. His passenger did the same. Castle joined them, leaned into the trunk, and hefted a package.

Tom keyed his mike. "All units—roll now! Go!"

It was a perfectly timed and choreographed movement on the part of the police. Two unmarked cars raced around the Bulldogger, one on each side, and skidded to a stop, the driver's side of each car facing the action and the vehicles themselves serving as a shield for the officers who scrambled out of the passenger sides and rested rifles and shotguns on the roofs. The drivers of each car lobbed a stun grenade toward the Buick before hustling out the passenger door. The concussive blasts came so close together that they sounded as one report, and the explosion was stunning, as was the eye-searing burst of white light.

Four men in black jackets marked "police" in large white letters charged around each side of the building on foot, assault rifles ready. They worked fast and they worked efficiently. In a matter of seconds, Craig, Castle, and their gunmen were flat on their faces in the swampy parking lot, hands cuffed behind their backs. Three of the men in jackets charged in the back door of the bar.

One of the black jackets waved to the warehouse window, performed a sweeping, theatrical bow, and then turned to stand guard over the prisoners. It was over.

"Perfect!" Tom laughed. "Absolutely perfect, and I got every bit of it. Not a shot fired!"

Julie, still dazed by the action below, could only nod.

A state trooper prisoner transport van pulled in behind the unmarked police vehicles. The suspects were hauled to their feet and marched into the van, under the close guard of transport personnel as well as the other police officers present. Two crime scene investigators were unloading the packages from the trunk of Craig's Buick, and a police photographer was taking shots of the area. Tom switched on the lights in the office, and the photographer swung his camera toward the warehouse and took several pictures showing the vantage point of the video setup.

Already the scene of the takedown was clearing. Police wreckers hooked on to Craig's car and the station wagon and hauled them away. The unmarked cars drove off sedately, like family sedans being driven to church on a Sunday morning, in direct contrast with the way they'd entered the scene.

Tom Davis was packing up his equipment, still smiling broadly.

"That was amazing," Julie said. "Thanks for letting me be here with you, Tom."

"I guess I'll see the story in the *News-Express* real soon," he said. "Glad to have you. One other thing—Ken asked me to give you this if everything went as we wanted it to." He held out a sealed business-sized envelope to her. "You better skedaddle, ma'am," he added. "There's going to be brass here soon, and I'd rather not have to explain you to them unless they ask me directly. If you're not here, they won't."

Julie took the envelope and put it in her purse, then held out her right hand to the technician. He took it and squeezed it lightly. "Take care, Tom," she said.

"You too, Julie."

She left the warehouse from the door she'd entered. The rain was still falling and showing no sign of abating. Puddles had formed in the gutters and were seeping into the streets. Julie sloshed to her truck parked on an adjacent side street and noticed how its red finish glistened under the streetlight. She didn't hurry through the downpour—she'd missed rain too much to scurry away from it, regardless of her hair and her clothing.

She sat behind her steering wheel and started her engine. She flicked on the interior light and used her thumbnail to open the slightly wet envelope and then unfolded the single handwritten page inside it.

Dear Julie—

I've very much enjoyed our time together. You're a great lady and a wonderful friend. You're a great reporter too, but I'm afraid you're not so hot as an actress.

Danny was in your heart every moment we spent together. When you kissed me the other night, you were kissing Danny, whether or not you fully realized it. But I didn't have to be a genius to see how much you cared for him. I tried to convince myself that wasn't true—but it is.

I wish both of you the best. I mean that, although it's a little hard to say it just now.

226

You wouldn't be reading this unless the
operation went very well. As I was setting things
up with the troopers, I was offered an undercover
position with them, predicated, of course, on
the outcome of the Craig/Castle takedown. I've
accepted that job. I'll be able to do lots of good
in the position. I'll be based out of Twin Buttes,
which is only a couple hundred miles from
Coldwater. So—maybe I'll be seeing you and
Danny before you know it.

Be well and happy, Julie.

Your friend,
Ken Townsend

Julie sat for several minutes, her own eyes shimmering as
much as the rain on her windshield. She took a crumpled
Kleenex out of her purse and blew her nose. Then she tugged
out her cell phone and punched a pre-entered number. She
listened as the number rang once and then again.

"Dr. Pulver. May I help you?"

"I'm sure you can, Danny. I'm about starved to death. Can
you meet me at the diner for a burger?"

When Danny finally spoke, his voice was slightly raspy.
"I'll meet you anywhere you want, any time you want, sweet-
heart. See you in ten minutes."

Before starting up her truck, Julie lowered her window
and stuck her hand outside, letting the rain fall softly on
her palm.

Watch for Book 3 in the
Montana Skies Series!

"Big Sky Country, my foot," Amy Hawkins grumbled as she watched sheets of rain skitter across the vast expanse of burgeoning grass that was her front lawn. When the lawn—the full two acres of it, including the front and the back—went in almost three weeks ago, the rain had started. At first, it was gentle and nurturing, and Amy welcomed it. Now it seemed like the sort of deluge Noah had faced, and the uniform drab gray of sodden day after sodden day was depressing. This certainly wasn't the glorious Montana weather that had brought her so eagerly to the state.

Amy stepped back from the window, and her foot found a home on the spiked tail of Nutsy, the kitten she'd adopted not a month before. Nutsy reacted as cats—regardless of age—do: he yowled with a wail that was far too big and too loud for his diminutive body, arched his back, hissed, and dashed off to cower under the couch, his favorite fortress against the confusing outer world.

A hissing streak of chain lightning flickered outside, followed immediately by a sharp crack like the report of a gun, which preceded the now-familiar hollow boom of thunder. Amy walked across her living room and stood gazing out of the picture window into her front yard. The house smelled new, as did the furniture, and the fine scent of the good wall-to-wall carpeting was still strong. She smiled at the aroma.

Amy, with an architect friend, had designed the house. It was modest-sized two bedroom, one and a half bath, but seemed like a luxury cottage to Amy after living the last few years in a small and terribly overpriced New York City apartment. Her parents' mansion in Connecticut, where she had spent her childhood, had always seemed like a cruise ship run aground—a look and a feeling Amy had strived to avoid in her new home.

Starting a new life is a great concept, Amy thought. *But is it possible at thirty-five?* She grinned. *It sure is—and I'm doing it.* A geographical change didn't eliminate or even alter the baggage of the past. All of that stayed solidly in place, she knew. But because the weight existed back there didn't mean it had to be hefted and carried every day. *Being an itinerant book editor and all that went with it was then—this is now.*

Confined too long by the weather to sit comfortably, Amy paced through her home like a lion in a cage. She stopped at the sliding glass doors off the kitchen and looked at her reflection in the glass. Her hair, brunette and shoulder length, framed a finely sculpted face—high cheekbones, a nice nose, and a generous, smiling mouth. And Amy considered her eyes—a rich, liquid brown—to be her best feature. Tall for a woman at five foot ten, Amy had decided early on not to give in to the tall girl stoop, the mildly hunched stance many taller girls opted for in order to appear shorter. That, Amy thought, made as much sense as a man calling attention to his baldness by wearing a cheap toupee.

Amy's laptop was on the kitchen table, where it'd rested since yesterday afternoon. As an editor now branching out into the world of writing fiction, she had few demands on her time other than those she imposed on herself. That was at least partially what the Montana move was all about—a place to see if the novel she'd fantasized about for years could actually turn into anything that might snare the reading public's attention.

The problem with all that, Amy admitted, was writer's block—a crippling state of mind for a writer that steps on creativity, joy in writing, and progress on a project. Amy had never actually believed in writer's block in the past. She'd attributed it to either fatigue or simple laziness on the part of the writer. Now, she realized, it was neither. It was a very real and quite frightening problem with which she now wrestled on a daily basis. Writer's block was doing a fine job of robbing her of sleep and casting shadows of self-doubt into her days. "I can beat this" had become a mantra-like affirmation, but it often felt to her like she was whistling as she passed a cemetery on a dark night, attempting to push away her fear.

Everything for her career change had clicked into place like the movement of a fine watch—at least until now. Her reputation as an editor—and three best sellers she'd worked on, two of which were made into major box-office hits—had gotten her a famous and very effective literary agent. Inheriting a significant amount of money from a great-aunt she had met a grand total of two times as a preteen had made the move and the home possible. The money, however, was finite, and Amy quickly learned that anything and everything having to do with building and furnishing a new home was astoundingly expensive. The advance on her novel her agent had been able to negotiate had been sizable—not in the six-figure range that heavyweights such as King and Updike garnered, but a good sum nevertheless. Now, though, her bank balance had dwindled to subsistence money, and the numbers kept her awake late at night. Her novel, she knew, could save her. But the way it was going . . . Amy shuddered.

A gust of wind slapped the side of the house. Amy smiled—not a window rattled. The rain continued to beat down, sweeping in gray sheets across her property and onto that of Jake Winters, her horse-farmer neighbor. *There's a strange one,* Amy thought. Perfectly content to ride around on his Quarter Horses and grow his thousand or so acres of hay, and live alone, except for the cowboys who worked for him. *Takes all kinds . . .*

Jake had ridden over when the construction people were digging Amy's basement and beginning her landscaping and introduced himself. He was a good-looking guy, maybe a couple of years older than her, who was dressed in a faded denim jacket, jeans, and boots. His eyes were a pale blue, which in some faces could have appeared weak or submissive. But the depth of Jake's tan and the strong line of his jaw made his eyes look open, friendly, almost mischievous somehow, as if only he knew the coming punch line of a joke.

"What are those fellows doing there?" Jake asked, pointing at a small backhoe that was digging a dog-house-sized pit every dozen feet or so and following a line of white twine attached to short metal rods stuck into the ground.

"I have a load of bushes coming in the next couple of days," Amy said. "They're going to follow the driveway up to the house."

"The bushes are already mature?" Jake asked. "Most folks buy seedlings and—"

He cut off the comment before finishing it.

"Patience isn't my strongest virtue," Amy said with a smile.

He met her smile with his own. "I can't say it's mine, either."

Jake let his eyes roam over Amy's property. "Fine piece of land. I didn't even know ol' man Woerner was selling it until I saw you up here walking around with the realtor from town." He shook his head, smiling. "Mr. Woerner never much cared for me since my friends and I tossed a string of cherry bombs into his privy one Halloween night a bunch of years ago."

"Wow! Those things are powerful. I hope there was no one in the privy at the time."

"No, there wasn't," Jake said. "I'll admit that it made a bit of a mess, though. Anyway, that's probably why Woerner didn't come to me when he wanted to sell."

233

"Would you have bought this parcel?" Amy asked.

"Well . . . probably. Yeah. I guess there's no such thing as owning too much land."

Jake's horse snorted, and he turned to the animal, whose reins he held loosely in his left hand. "I'd better get this boy home," he said. "I have chores waiting." He stepped into a stirrup and swung easily into his western saddle. "Do you ride?"

"Not since a pony ride on my sixth birthday," Amy said.

Jake grinned. "I have an ol' mare I can put you on who's a pussycat. If you like, we can go out on horseback, and I can show you around a bit. There're Indian burial grounds not far from here that not many know about. Maybe you'd like to see them."

"I'd love to, Jake. Let's do that."

He nodded. "Good, then. See you soon." He turned his horse away from Amy and loped off toward his own land, the hooves of his horse thunking heavily on the soil, steel shoes tossing an occasional divot into the air behind them.

DON'T MISS BOOK ONE IN THE

MONTANA SKIES TRILOGY

CHANGES *of* HEART

PAIGE LEE
ELLISTON

MONTANA SKIES

ℛ Revell